THE PRINCE

Niccolò Machiavelli

THE PRINCE

Translated by
W. K. Marriott

W. Books

This is a W. Books publication, a division of Grupo Ciranda Cultural.

Text: Niccolò Machiavelli
First Publication: 1532
Translation: W. K. Marriott
Graphic Design: Linea Editora
Cover: Chama Studio

Dados Internacionais de Catalogação na Publicação (CIP) de acordo com ISBD

M149t Machiavelli, Niccolo.

The Prince / Niccolo Machiavelli. - Jandira, SP : W. Books, 2025.
160 p. : 12,80cm x 19,70cm. - (Classics).

ISBN: 978-65-83398-56-7

1. Ciências políticas. 2. Sucesso. 3. Crescimento. 4. Pensamentos. 5. Estratégia. I. Título. II. Série.

2024-2311 CDD 320
CDU 32

Elaborada por Lucio Feitosa - CRB-8/8803

Índice para catálogo sistemático:
1. Ciências políticas 320
2. Ciências políticas 32

www.cirandacultural.com.br

Contents

Nicolo Machiavelli, born at Florence on 3rd May 1469. From 1494 to 1512 held an official post at Florence which included diplomatic missions to various European courts. Imprisoned in Florence, 1512; later exiled and returned to San Casciano. Died at Florence on 22nd June 1527.

INTRODUCTION

Nicolo Machiavelli was born at Florence on 3rd May 1469. He was the second son of Bernardo di Nicolo Machiavelli, a lawyer of some repute, and of Bartolommea di Stefano Nelli, his wife. Both parents were members of the old Florentine nobility.

His life falls naturally into three periods, each of which singularly enough constitutes a distinct and important era in the history of Florence. His youth was concurrent with the greatness of Florence as an Italian power under the guidance of Lorenzo de' Medici, Il Magnifico. The downfall of the Medici in Florence occurred in 1494, in which year Machiavelli entered the public service. During his official career Florence was free under the government of a Republic, which lasted until 1512, when the Medici returned to power, and Machiavelli lost his office. The Medici again ruled Florence from 1512 until 1527, when they were once more driven out. This was the period of Machiavelli's literary activity and increasing influence; but he died, within a few weeks of the expulsion of the Medici, on 22nd June 1527, in his fifty-eighth year, without having regained office.

YOUTH — Æt. 1-25—1469-94

Although there is little recorded of the youth of Machiavelli, the Florence of those days is so well known that the early environment of this representative citizen may be easily imagined. Florence has been described as a city with two opposite currents of life, one directed by the fervent and austere Savonarola, the other by the splendour-loving Lorenzo. Savonarola's influence upon the young

Machiavelli must have been slight, for although at one time he wielded immense power over the fortunes of Florence, he only furnished Machiavelli with a subject of a gibe in *The Prince*, where he is cited as an example of an unarmed prophet who came to a bad end. Whereas the magnificence of the Medicean rule during the life of Lorenzo appeared to have impressed Machiavelli strongly, for he frequently recurs to it in his writings, and it is to Lorenzo's grandson that he dedicates *The Prince*.

Machiavelli, in his "History of Florence," gives us a picture of the young men among whom his youth was passed. He writes: "They were freer than their forefathers in dress and living, and spent more in other kinds of excesses, consuming their time and money in idleness, gaming, and women; their chief aim was to appear well dressed and to speak with wit and acuteness, whilst he who could wound others the most cleverly was thought the wisest." In a letter to his son Guido, Machiavelli shows why youth should avail itself of its opportunities for study, and leads us to infer that his own youth had been so occupied. He writes: "I have received your letter, which has given me the greatest pleasure, especially because you tell me you are quite restored in health, than which I could have no better news; for if God grant life to you, and to me, I hope to make a good man of you if you are willing to do your share." Then, writing of a new patron, he continues: "This will turn out well for you, but it is necessary for you to study; since, then, you have no longer the excuse of illness, take pains to study letters and music, for you see what honour is done to me for the little skill I have. Therefore, my son, if you wish to please me, and to bring success and honour to yourself, do right and study, because others will help you if you help yourself."

OFFICE — Æt. 25-43—1494-1512

The second period of Machiavelli's life was spent in the service of the free Republic of Florence, which flourished, as stated above, from the expulsion of the Medici in 1494 until their return in 1512. After serving four years in one of the public offices he was appointed Chancellor and Secretary to the Second Chancery, the Ten of Liberty and Peace. Here we are on firm ground when dealing with the events of Machiavelli's life, for during this time he took a leading part in the affairs of the Republic, and we have its decrees, records, and dispatches to guide us, as well as his own writings. A mere recapitulation of a few of his transactions with the statesmen and soldiers of his time gives a fair indication of his activities, and supplies the sources from which he drew the experiences and characters which illustrate *The Prince*.

His first mission was in 1499 to Catherina Sforza, "my lady of Forli" of *The Prince*, from whose conduct and fate he drew the moral that it is far better to earn the confidence of the people than to rely on fortresses. This is a very noticeable principle in Machiavelli, and is urged by him in many ways as a matter of vital importance to princes.

In 1500 he was sent to France to obtain terms from Louis XII for continuing the war against Pisa: this king it was who, in his conduct of affairs in Italy, committed the five capital errors in statecraft summarized in *The Prince*, and was consequently driven out. He, also, it was who made the dissolution of his marriage a condition of support to Pope Alexander VI; which leads Machiavelli to refer those who urge that such promises should be kept to what he has written concerning the faith of princes.

Machiavelli's public life was largely occupied with events arising out of the ambitions of Pope Alexander VI and his son, Cesare Borgia, the Duke Valentino, and these characters fill a large space of *The Prince*. Machiavelli never hesitates to cite the actions of the duke for the benefit of usurpers who wish to keep the states they have seized; he can, indeed, find no precepts to offer so good as the pattern of Cesare Borgia's conduct, insomuch that Cesare is acclaimed by some critics as the "hero" of *The Prince*. Yet in *The Prince* the duke is in point of fact cited as a type of the man who rises on the fortune of others, and falls with them; who takes every course that might be expected from a prudent man but the course which will save him; who is prepared for all eventualities but the one which happens; and who, when all his abilities fail to carry him through, exclaims that it was not his fault, but an extraordinary and unforeseen fatality.

On the death of Pius III, in 1503, Machiavelli was sent to Rome to watch the election of his successor, and there he saw Cesare Borgia cheated into allowing the choice of the College to fall on Giuliano delle Rovere (Julius II), who was one of the cardinals that had most reason to fear the duke. Machiavelli, when commenting on this election, says that he who thinks new favours will cause great personages to forget old injuries deceives himself. Julius did not rest until he had ruined Cesare.

It was to Julius II that Machiavelli was sent in 1506, when that pontiff was commencing his enterprise against Bologna; which he brought to a successful issue, as he did many of his other adventures, owing chiefly to his impetuous character. It is in reference to Pope Julius that Machiavelli moralizes on the resemblance between Fortune and women, and concludes that it is the bold rather than the cautious man that will win and hold them both.

It is impossible to follow here the varying fortunes of the Italian states, which in 1507 were controlled by France, Spain, and Germany, with results that have lasted to our day; we are concerned with those events, and with the three great actors in them, so far only as they impinge on the personality of Machiavelli. He had several meetings with Louis XII of France, and his estimate of that monarch's character has already been alluded to. Machiavelli has painted Ferdinand of Aragon as the man who accomplished great things under the cloak of religion, but who in reality had no mercy, faith, humanity, or integrity; and who, had he allowed himself to be influenced by such motives, would have been ruined. The Emperor Maximilian was one of the most interesting men of the age, and his character has been drawn by many hands; but Machiavelli, who was an envoy at his court in 1507-8, reveals the secret of his many failures when he describes him as a secretive man, without force of character—ignoring the human agencies necessary to carry his schemes into effect, and never insisting on the fulfilment of his wishes.

The remaining years of Machiavelli's official career were filled with events arising out of the League of Cambrai, made in 1508 between the three great European powers already mentioned and the pope, with the object of crushing the Venetian Republic. This result was attained in the battle of Vaila, when Venice lost in one day all that she had won in eight hundred years. Florence had a difficult part to play during these events, complicated as they were by the feud which broke out between the pope and the French, because friendship with France had dictated the entire policy of the Republic. When, in 1511, Julius II finally formed the Holy League against France, and with the assistance of the Swiss drove the French out of Italy, Florence lay at the mercy of the Pope, and had to submit to his terms, one of which was that the Medici should be restored. The return of the Medici to Florence on 1st September 1512, and the consequent fall of the Republic, was the signal for the dismissal of Machiavelli and his friends, and thus put an end to his public career, for, as we have seen, he died without regaining office.

LITERATURE AND DEATH — Æt. 43-58—1512-27

On the return of the Medici, Machiavelli, who for a few weeks had vainly hoped to retain his office under the new masters of Florence, was dismissed by decree dated 7th November 1512. Shortly after this he was accused of complicity in an abortive conspiracy against the Medici, imprisoned, and put to the question by torture. The new Medicean pope, Leo X, procured his release, and he retired to his small property at San Casciano, near Florence, where he devoted himself to literature. In a letter to Francesco Vettori, dated 13th December 1513, he has left a very interesting description of his life at this period, which elucidates his methods and his motives in writing *The Prince*. After describing his daily occupations with his family and neighbours, he writes: "The evening being come, I return home and go to my study; at the entrance I pull off my peasant-clothes, covered with dust and dirt, and put on my noble court dress, and thus becomingly re-clothed I pass into the ancient courts of the men of old, where, being lovingly received by them, I am fed with that food which is mine alone; where I do not hesitate to speak with them, and to ask for the reason of their actions, and they in their benignity answer me; and for four hours I feel no weariness, I forget every trouble, poverty does not dismay, death does not terrify me; I am possessed entirely by those great men. And because Dante says:

> *Knowledge doth come of learning well retained,*
> *Unfruitful else,*

I have noted down what I have gained from their conversation, and have composed a small work on 'Principalities,' where I pour myself out as fully as I can in meditation on the subject, discussing what a principality is, what kinds there are, how they can be acquired, how they can be kept, why they are lost: and if any of my fancies ever pleased you, this ought not to displease you: and to a prince, especially to a new one, it should be welcome: therefore I dedicate it to his Magnificence Giuliano. Filippo Casavecchio has seen it; he will be able to tell you what is in it, and of the discourses I have had with him; nevertheless, I am still enriching and polishing it."

The "little book" suffered many vicissitudes before attaining the form in which it has reached us. Various mental influences were at work during its composition; its title and patron were changed; and for some unknown reason it was finally dedicated to Lorenzo de' Medici. Although Machiavelli discussed with Casavecchio whether it should be sent or presented in person to the patron, there is no evidence that Lorenzo ever received or even read it: he certainly never gave Machiavelli any employment. Although it was plagiarized during Machiavelli's lifetime, *The Prince* was never published by him, and its text is still disputable.

Machiavelli concludes his letter to Vettori thus: "And as to this little thing [his book], when it has been read it will be seen that during the fifteen years I have given to the study of statecraft I have neither slept nor idled; and men ought ever to desire to be served by one who has reaped experience at the expense of others. And of my loyalty none could doubt, because having always kept faith I could not now learn how to break it; for he who has been faithful and honest, as I have, cannot change his nature; and my poverty is a witness to my honesty."

Before Machiavelli had got *The Prince* off his hands he commenced his "Discourse on the First Decade of Titus Livius," which should be read concurrently with *The Prince*. These and several minor works occupied him until the year 1518, when he accepted a small commission to look after the affairs of some Florentine merchants at Genoa. In 1519 the Medicean rulers of Florence granted a few political concessions to her citizens, and Machiavelli with others was consulted upon a new constitution under which the Great Council was to be restored; but on one pretext or another it was not promulgated.

In 1520 the Florentine merchants again had recourse to Machiavelli to settle their difficulties with Lucca, but this year was chiefly remarkable for his re-entry into Florentine literary society, where he was much sought after, and also for the production of his "Art of War." It was in the same year that he received a commission at the instance of Cardinal de' Medici to write the "History of Florence," a task which occupied him until 1525. His return to popular favour may have determined the Medici to give him this employment, for an old writer observes that "an able statesman out of work, like a huge whale, will endeavour to overturn the ship unless he has an empty cask to play with."

When the "History of Florence" was finished, Machiavelli took it to Rome for presentation to his patron, Giuliano de' Medici, who had in the meanwhile become pope under the title of Clement VII. It is somewhat remarkable that, as, in 1513, Machiavelli had written *The Prince* for the instruction of the Medici after they had just regained power in Florence, so, in 1525, he dedicated the "History of Florence" to the head of the family when its ruin was now at hand. In that year the battle of Pavia destroyed the French rule in Italy, and left Francis I a prisoner in the hands of his great rival, Charles V. This was followed by the sack of Rome, upon the news of which the popular party at Florence threw off the yoke of the Medici, who were once more banished.

Machiavelli was absent from Florence at this time, but hastened his return, hoping to secure his former office of secretary to the "Ten of Liberty and Peace." Unhappily he was taken ill soon after he reached Florence, where he died on 22nd June 1527.

THE MAN AND HIS WORKS

No one can say where the bones of Machiavelli rest, but modern Florence has decreed him a stately cenotaph in Santa Croce, by the side of her most famous sons; recognizing that, whatever other nations may have found in his works, Italy found in them the idea of her unity and the germs of her renaissance among the nations of Europe. Whilst it is idle to protest against the world-wide and evil signification of his name, it may be pointed out that the harsh construction of his doctrine which this sinister reputation implies was unknown to his own day, and that the researches of recent times have enabled us to interpret him more reasonably. It is due to these inquiries that the shape of an "unholy necromancer," which so long haunted men's vision, has begun to fade.

Machiavelli was undoubtedly a man of great observation, acuteness, and industry; noting with appreciative eye whatever passed before him, and with his supreme literary gift turning it to account in his enforced retirement from affairs. He does not present himself, nor is he depicted by his contemporaries, as a type of that rare combination, the successful statesman and author, for he appears to have been only moderately prosperous in his several embassies and political employments. He was misled by Catherina Sforza, ignored by Louis XII, overawed by Cesare Borgia; several of his embassies were quite barren of results; his attempts to fortify Florence failed, and the soldiery that he raised astonished everybody by their cowardice. In the conduct of his own affairs he was timid and time-serving; he dared not appear by the side of Soderini, to whom he owed so much, for fear of compromising himself; his connection with the Medici was open to suspicion, and Giuliano appears to have recognized his real forte when he set him to write the "History of Florence," rather than employ him in the state. And it is on the literary side of his character, and there alone, that we find no weakness and no failure.

Although the light of almost four centuries has been focused on *The Prince*, its problems are still debatable and interesting, because they are the eternal problems between the ruled and their rulers. Such as they are, its ethics are those of Machiavelli's contemporaries; yet they cannot be said to be out of date so long as the governments of Europe rely on material rather than on moral forces. Its historical incidents and personages become interesting by reason of the uses which Machiavelli makes of them to illustrate his theories of government and conduct.

Leaving out of consideration those maxims of state which still furnish some European and eastern statesmen with principles of action, *The Prince* is bestrewn with truths that can be proved at every turn. Men are still the dupes of their simplicity and greed, as they were in the days of Alexander VI. The cloak of religion still conceals the vices which Machiavelli laid bare in the character of Ferdinand of Aragon. Men will not look at things as they really are, but as they wish them to be—and are ruined. In politics there are no perfectly safe courses; prudence consists in choosing the least dangerous ones. Then—to pass to a higher plane—Machiavelli reiterates that, although crimes may win an empire, they do not win glory. Necessary wars are just wars, and the arms of a nation are hallowed when it has no other resource but to fight.

It is the cry of a far later day than Machiavelli's that government should be elevated into a living moral force, capable of inspiring the people with a just recognition of the fundamental principles of society; to this "high argument" *The Prince* contributes but little. Machiavelli always refused to write either of men or of governments otherwise than as he found them, and he writes with such skill and insight that his work is of abiding value. But what invests *The Prince* with more than a merely artistic or historical interest is the incontrovertible truth that it deals with the great principles which still guide nations and rulers in their relationship with each other and their neighbours.

In translating *The Prince* my aim has been to achieve at all costs an exact literal rendering of the original, rather than a fluent paraphrase adapted to the modern notions of style and expression. Machiavelli was no facile phrasemonger; the conditions under which he wrote obliged him to weigh every word; his themes were lofty, his substance grave, his manner nobly plain and serious. *Quis eo fuit unquam in partiundis rebus, in definiendis, in explanandis pressior?* In *The Prince*, it may be truly said, there is reason assignable, not only for every word, but for the position of every word. To an Englishman of Shakespeare's time the translation of such a treatise was in some ways a comparatively easy task, for in those times the genius of the English more nearly resembled that of the Italian language; to the Englishman of to-day it is not so simple. To take a single example: the word *intrattenere*, employed by Machiavelli to indicate the policy adopted by the Roman Senate towards the weaker states of Greece, would by an Elizabethan be correctly rendered "entertain," and every contemporary reader would understand what was meant by saying that "Rome *entertained* the Ætolians and the Achaeans without augmenting their power." But to-day such a phrase would seem obsolete and ambiguous, if not unmeaning: we are compelled to say that

"Rome maintained friendly relations with the Ætolians," etc., using four words to do the work of one. I have tried to preserve the pithy brevity of the Italian so far as was consistent with an absolute fidelity to the sense. If the result be an occasional asperity I can only hope that the reader, in his eagerness to reach the author's meaning, may overlook the roughness of the road that leads him to it.

The following is a list of the works of Machiavelli:

Principal works. Discorso sopra le cose di Pisa, 1499; Del modo di trattare i popoli della Valdichiana ribellati, 1502; Del modo tenuto dal duca Valentino nell' ammazzare Vitellozzo Vitelli, Oliverotto da Fermo, etc., 1502; Discorso sopra la provisione del danaro, 1502; Decennale primo (poem in terza rima), 1506; Ritratti delle cose dell' Alemagna, 1508-12; Decennale secondo, 1509; Ritratti delle cose di Francia, 1510; Discorsi sopra la prima deca di T. Livio, 3 vols., 1512-17; Il Principe, 1513; Andria, comedy translated from Terence, 1513 (?); Mandragola, prose comedy in five acts, with prologue in verse, 1513; Della lingua (dialogue), 1514; Clizia, comedy in prose, 1515 (?); Belfagor arcidiavolo (novel), 1515; Asino d'oro (poem in terza rima), 1517; Dell' arte della guerra, 1519-20; Discorso sopra il riformare lo stato di Firenze, 1520; Sommario delle cose della citta di Lucca, 1520; Vita di Castruccio Castracani da Lucca, 1520; Istorie fiorentine, 8 books, 1521-5; Frammenti storici, 1525.

Other poems include Sonetti, Canzoni, Ottave, and Canti carnascialeschi.

Editions. Aldo, Venice, 1546; della Tertina, 1550; Cambiagi, Florence, 6 vols., 1782-5; dei Classici, Milan, 10 1813; Silvestri, 9 vols., 1820-2; Passerini, Fanfani, Milanesi, 6 vols. only published, 1873-7.

Minor works. Ed. F. L. Polidori, 1852; Lettere familiari, ed. E. Alvisi, 1883, 2 editions, one with excisions; Credited Writings, ed. G. Canestrini, 1857; Letters to F. Vettori, see A. Ridolfi, Pensieri intorno allo scopo di N. Machiavelli nel libro Il Principe, etc.; D. Ferrara, The Private Correspondence of Nicolo Machiavelli, 1929.

DEDICATION

To the Magnificent Lorenzo Di Piero De' Medici

Those who strive to obtain the good graces of a prince are accustomed to come before him with such things as they hold most precious, or in which they see him take most delight; whence one often sees horses, arms, cloth of gold, precious stones, and similar ornaments presented to princes, worthy of their greatness.

Desiring therefore to present myself to your Magnificence with some testimony of my devotion towards you, I have not found among my possessions anything which I hold more dear than, or value so much as, the knowledge of the actions of great men, acquired by long experience in contemporary affairs, and a continual study of antiquity; which, having reflected upon it with great and prolonged diligence, I now send, digested into a little volume, to your Magnificence.

And although I may consider this work unworthy of your countenance, nevertheless I trust much to your benignity that it may be acceptable, seeing that it is not possible for me to make a better gift than to offer you the opportunity of understanding in the shortest time all that I have learnt in so many years, and with so many troubles and dangers; which work I have not embellished with swelling or magnificent words, nor stuffed with rounded periods, nor with any extrinsic allurements or adornments whatever, with which so many are accustomed to embellish their works; for I have wished either that no honour should be given it, or else that the truth of the matter and the weightiness of the theme shall make it acceptable.

Nor do I hold with those who regard it as a presumption if a man of low and humble condition dare to discuss and settle the concerns of princes; because, just as those who draw landscapes place themselves below in the plain to contemplate the nature of the mountains and of lofty places, and in order to contemplate the plains place themselves upon high mountains, even so to understand the nature of the people it needs to be a prince, and to understand that of princes it needs to be of the people.

Take then, your Magnificence, this little gift in the spirit in which I send it; wherein, if it be diligently read and considered by you, you will learn my extreme desire that you should attain that greatness which fortune and your other attributes promise. And if your Magnificence from the summit of your greatness will sometimes turn your eyes to these lower regions, you will see how unmeritedly I suffer a great and continued malignity of fortune.

The Prince

Chapter I
HOW MANY KINDS OF PRINCIPALITIES THERE ARE, AND BY WHAT MEANS THEY ARE ACQUIRED

All states, all powers, that have held and hold rule over men have been and are either republics or principalities.

Principalities are either hereditary, in which the family has been long established; or they are new.

The new are either entirely new, as was Milan to Francesco Sforza, or they are, as it were, members annexed to the hereditary state of the prince who has acquired them, as was the kingdom of Naples to that of the King of Spain.

Such dominions thus acquired are either accustomed to live under a prince, or to live in freedom; and are acquired either by the arms of the prince himself, or of others, or else by fortune or by ability.

Chapter II
CONCERNING HEREDITARY PRINCIPALITIES

I will leave out all discussion on republics, inasmuch as in another place I have written of them at length, and will address myself only to principalities. In doing so I will keep to the order indicated above, and discuss how such principalities are to be ruled and preserved.

I say at once there are fewer difficulties in holding hereditary states, and those long accustomed to the family of their prince, than new ones; for it is sufficient only not to transgress the customs of his ancestors, and to deal prudently with circumstances as they arise, for a prince of average powers to maintain himself in his state, unless he be deprived of it by some extraordinary and excessive force; and if he should be so deprived of it, whenever anything sinister happens to the usurper, he will regain it.

We have in Italy, for example, the Duke of Ferrara, who could not have withstood the attacks of the Venetians in '84, nor those of Pope Julius in '10, unless he had been long established in his dominions. For the hereditary prince has less cause and less necessity to offend; hence it happens that he will be more loved; and unless extraordinary vices cause him to be hated, it is reasonable to expect that his subjects will be naturally well disposed towards him; and in the antiquity and duration of his rule the memories and motives that make for change are lost, for one change always leaves the toothing for another.

Chapter III
CONCERNING MIXED PRINCIPALITIES

But the difficulties occur in a new principality. And firstly, if it be not entirely new, but is, as it were, a member of a state which, taken collectively, may be called composite, the changes arise chiefly from an inherent difficulty which there is in all new principalities; for men change their rulers willingly, hoping to better themselves, and this hope induces them to take up arms against him who rules: wherein they are deceived, because they afterwards find by experience they have gone from bad to worse. This follows also on another natural and common necessity, which always causes a new prince to burden those who have submitted to him with his soldiery and with infinite other hardships which he must put upon his new acquisition.

In this way you have enemies in all those whom you have injured in seizing that principality, and you are not able to keep those friends who put you there because of your not being able to satisfy them in the way they expected, and you cannot take strong measures against them, feeling bound to them. For, although one may be very strong in armed forces, yet in entering a province one has always need of the goodwill of the natives.

For these reasons Louis the Twelfth, King of France, quickly occupied Milan, and as quickly lost it; and to turn him out the first time it only needed Lodovico's own forces; because those who had opened the gates to him, finding themselves deceived in their hopes of future benefit, would not endure the ill-treatment of the new prince. It is very true that, after acquiring rebellious provinces a second time, they are not so lightly lost afterwards, because the prince, with little reluctance, takes the opportunity of the rebellion to punish the delinquents, to clear out the suspects, and to strengthen himself in the weakest places. Thus to cause France to lose Milan the first time it was enough for the Duke Lodovico[1] to raise insurrections on the borders; but to cause him to lose it a second time it was necessary to bring the whole world against him, and that his armies should be defeated and driven out of Italy; which followed from the causes above mentioned.

Nevertheless Milan was taken from France both the first and the second time. The general reasons for the first have been discussed; it remains to name those for the second, and to see what resources he had, and what any one in his situation would have had for maintaining himself more securely in his acquisition than did the King of France.

Now I say that those dominions which, when acquired, are added to an ancient state by him who acquires them, are either of the same country and language, or they are not. When they are, it is easier to hold them, especially when they have not been accustomed to self-government; and to hold them securely it is enough to have destroyed the family of the prince who was ruling them; because the two peoples, preserving in other things the old conditions, and not being unlike in customs, will live quietly together, as one has seen in Brittany, Burgundy, Gascony, and Normandy, which have been bound to France for so long a time: and, although there may be some difference in language, nevertheless the customs are alike, and the people will easily be able to get on amongst themselves. He who has annexed them, if he wishes to hold them, has only to bear in mind two considerations: the one, that the family of their former lord is extinguished; the other, that neither their laws nor their taxes are altered, so that in a very short time they will become entirely one body with the old principality.

---

[1] Duke Lodovico was Lodovico Moro, a son of Francesco Sforza, who married Beatrice d'Este. He ruled over Milan from 1494 to 1500, and died in 1510.

But when states are acquired in a country differing in language, customs, or laws, there are difficulties, and good fortune and great energy are needed to hold them, and one of the greatest and most real helps would be that he who has acquired them should go and reside there. This would make his position more secure and durable, as it has made that of the Turk in Greece, who, notwithstanding all the other measures taken by him for holding that state, if he had not settled there, would not have been able to keep it. Because, if one is on the spot, disorders are seen as they spring up, and one can quickly remedy them; but if one is not at hand, they are heard of only when they are great, and then one can no longer remedy them. Besides this, the country is not pillaged by your officials; the subjects are satisfied by prompt recourse to the prince; thus, wishing to be good, they have more cause to love him, and wishing to be otherwise, to fear him. He who would attack that state from the outside must have the utmost caution; as long as the prince resides there it can only be wrested from him with the greatest difficulty.

The other and better course is to send colonies to one or two places, which may be as keys to that state, for it is necessary either to do this or else to keep there a great number of cavalry and infantry. A prince does not spend much on colonies, for with little or no expense he can send them out and keep them there, and he offends a minority only of the citizens from whom he takes lands and houses to give them to the new inhabitants; and those whom he offends, remaining poor and scattered, are never able to injure him; whilst the rest being uninjured are easily kept quiet, and at the same time are anxious not to err for fear it should happen to them as it has to those who have been despoiled. In conclusion, I say that these colonies are not costly, they are more faithful, they injure less, and the injured, as has been said, being poor and scattered, cannot hurt. Upon this, one has to remark that men ought either to be well treated or crushed, because they can avenge themselves of lighter injuries, of more serious ones they cannot; therefore the injury that is to be done to a man ought to be of such a kind that one does not stand in fear of revenge.

But in maintaining armed men there in place of colonies one spends much more, having to consume on the garrison all the income from the state, so that the acquisition turns into a loss, and many more are exasperated, because the whole state is injured; through the shifting of the garrison up and down all become acquainted with hardship, and all become hostile, and they are enemies who, whilst beaten on their own ground, are yet able to do hurt. For every reason, therefore, such guards are as useless as a colony is useful.

Again, the prince who holds a country differing in the above respects ought to make himself the head and defender of his less powerful neighbours, and to weaken the more powerful amongst them, taking care that no foreigner as powerful as himself shall, by any accident, get a footing there; for it will always happen that such a one will be introduced by those who are discontented, either through excess of ambition or through fear, as one has seen already. The Romans were brought into Greece by the Ætolians; and in every other country where they obtained a footing they were brought in by the inhabitants. And the usual course of affairs is that, as soon as a powerful foreigner enters a country, all the subject states are drawn to him, moved by the hatred which they feel against the ruling power. So that in respect to those subject states he has not to take any trouble to gain them over to himself, for the whole of them quickly rally to the state which he has acquired there. He has only to take care that they do not get hold of too much power and too much authority, and then with his own forces, and with their goodwill, he can easily keep down the more powerful of them, so as to remain entirely master in the country. And he who does not properly manage this business will soon lose what he has acquired, and whilst he does hold it he will have endless difficulties and troubles.

The Romans, in the countries which they annexed, observed closely these measures; they sent colonies and maintained friendly relations with[2] the minor powers, without increasing their strength;

---

[2] See remark in the introduction on the word "intrattenere."

they kept down the greater, and did not allow any strong foreign powers to gain authority. Greece appears to me sufficient for an example. The Achaeans and Ætolians were kept friendly by them, the kingdom of Macedonia was humbled, Antiochus was driven out; yet the merits of the Achaeans and Ætolians never secured for them permission to increase their power, nor did the persuasions of Philip ever induce the Romans to be his friends without first humbling him, nor did the influence of Antiochus make them agree that he should retain any lordship over the country. Because the Romans did in these instances what all prudent princes ought to do, who have to regard not only present troubles, but also future ones, for which they must prepare with every energy, because, when foreseen, it is easy to remedy them; but if you wait until they approach, the medicine is no longer in time because the malady has become incurable; for it happens in this, as the physicians say it happens in hectic fever, that in the beginning of the malady it is easy to cure but difficult to detect, but in the course of time, not having been either detected or treated in the beginning, it becomes easy to detect but difficult to cure. Thus it happens in affairs of state, for when the evils that arise have been foreseen (which it is only given to a wise man to see), they can be quickly redressed, but when, through not having been foreseen, they have been permitted to grow in a way that every one can see them, there is no longer a remedy. Therefore, the Romans, foreseeing troubles, dealt with them at once, and, even to avoid a war, would not let them come to a head, for they knew that war is not to be avoided, but is only to be put off to the advantage of others; moreover they wished to fight with Philip and Antiochus in Greece so as not to have to do it in Italy; they could have avoided both, but this they did not wish; nor did that ever please them which is forever in the mouths of the wise ones of our time:—Let us enjoy the benefits of the time—but rather the benefits of their own valour and prudence, for time drives everything before it, and is able to bring with it good as well as evil, and evil as well as good.

But let us turn to France and inquire whether she has done any of the things mentioned. I will speak of Louis[3] (and not of Charles)[4] as the one whose conduct is the better to be observed, he having held possession of Italy for the longest period; and you will see that he has done the opposite to those things which ought to be done to retain a state composed of divers elements.

King Louis was brought into Italy by the ambition of the Venetians, who desired to obtain half the state of Lombardy by his intervention. I will not blame the course taken by the king, because, wishing to get a foothold in Italy, and having no friends there—seeing rather that every door was shut to him owing to the conduct of Charles—he was forced to accept those friendships which he could get, and he would have succeeded very quickly in his design if in other matters he had not made some mistakes. The king, however, having acquired Lombardy, regained at once the authority which Charles had lost: Genoa yielded; the Florentines became his friends; the Marquess of Mantua, the Duke of Ferrara, the Bentivogli, my lady of Forli, the Lords of Faenza, of Pesaro, of Rimini, of Camerino, of Piombino, the Lucchese, the Pisans, the Sienese—everybody made advances to him to become his friend. Then could the Venetians realize the rashness of the course taken by them, which, in order that they might secure two towns in Lombardy, had made the king master of two-thirds of Italy.

Let any one now consider with what little difficulty the king could have maintained his position in Italy had he observed the rules above laid down, and kept all his friends secure and protected; for although they were numerous they were both weak and timid, some afraid of the Church, some of the Venetians, and thus they would always have been forced to stand in with him, and by their means he could easily have made himself secure against those who remained powerful. But he was no sooner in Milan than he did the contrary by assisting Pope Alexander to occupy the Romagna. It never occurred

---

3 Louis XII, King of France, "The Father of the People," born 1462, died 1515.

4 Charles VIII, King of France, born 1470, died 1498.

to him that by this action he was weakening himself, depriving himself of friends and of those who had thrown themselves into his lap, whilst he aggrandized the Church by adding much temporal power to the spiritual, thus giving it greater authority. And having committed this prime error, he was obliged to follow it up, so much so that, to put an end to the ambition of Alexander, and to prevent his becoming the master of Tuscany, he was himself forced to come into Italy.

And as if it were not enough to have aggrandized the Church, and deprived himself of friends, he, wishing to have the kingdom of Naples, divided it with the King of Spain, and where he was the prime arbiter in Italy he takes an associate, so that the ambitious of that country and the malcontents of his own should have somewhere to shelter; and whereas he could have left in the kingdom his own pensioner as king, he drove him out, to put one there who was able to drive him, Louis, out in turn.

The wish to acquire is in truth very natural and common, and men always do so when they can, and for this they will be praised not blamed; but when they cannot do so, yet wish to do so by any means, then there is folly and blame. Therefore, if France could have attacked Naples with her own forces she ought to have done so; if she could not, then she ought not to have divided it. And if the partition which she made with the Venetians in Lombardy was justified by the excuse that by it she got a foothold in Italy, this other partition merited blame, for it had not the excuse of that necessity.

Therefore Louis made these five errors: he destroyed the minor powers, he increased the strength of one of the greater powers in Italy, he brought in a foreign power, he did not settle in the country, he did not send colonies. Which errors, had he lived, were not enough to injure him had he not made a sixth by taking away their dominions from the Venetians; because, had he not aggrandized the Church, nor brought Spain into Italy, it would have been very reasonable and necessary to humble them; but having first taken these steps, he ought never to have consented to their ruin, for they, being powerful, would always have kept off others from designs on Lombardy, to which the Venetians would never have consented except to become masters themselves there; also because the others would not wish to take Lombardy from France in order to give it to the Venetians, and to run counter to both they would not have had the courage.

And if any one should say: "King Louis yielded the Romagna to Alexander and the kingdom to Spain to avoid war," I answer for the reasons given above that a blunder ought never to be perpetrated to avoid war, because it is not to be avoided, but is only deferred to your disadvantage. And if another should allege the pledge which the king had given to the Pope that he would assist him in the enterprise, in exchange for the dissolution of his marriage[5] and for the cap to Rouen,[6] to that I reply what I shall write later on concerning the faith of princes, and how it ought to be kept.

Thus King Louis lost Lombardy by not having followed any of the conditions observed by those who have taken possession of countries and wished to retain them. Nor is there any miracle in this, but much that is reasonable and quite natural. And on these matters I spoke at Nantes with Rouen, when Valentino, as Cesare Borgia, the son of Pope Alexander, was usually called, occupied the Romagna, and on Cardinal Rouen observing to me that the Italians did not understand war, I replied to him that the French did not understand statecraft, meaning that otherwise they would not have allowed the Church to reach such greatness. And in fact it has been seen that the greatness of the Church and of Spain in Italy has been caused by France, and her ruin may be attributed to them. From this a general rule is drawn which never or rarely fails: that he who is the cause of another becoming powerful is ruined; because that predominancy has been brought about either by astuteness or else by force, and both are distrusted by him who has been raised to power.

---

[5] Louis XII divorced his wife, Jeanne, daughter of Louis XI, and married in 1499 Anne of Brittany, widow of Charles VIII, in order to retain the Duchy of Brittany for the crown.

[6] The Archbishop of Rouen. He was Georges d'Amboise, created a cardinal by Alexander VI. Born 1460, died 1510.

Chapter IV
WHY THE KINGDOM OF DARIUS, CONQUERED BY ALEXANDER, DID NOT REBEL AGAINST THE SUCCESSORS OF ALEXANDER AT HIS DEATH

Considering the difficulties which men have had to hold to a newly acquired state, some might wonder how, seeing that Alexander the Great became the master of Asia in a few years, and died whilst it was scarcely settled (whence it might appear reasonable that the whole empire would have rebelled), nevertheless his successors maintained themselves, and had to meet no other difficulty than that which arose among themselves from their own ambitions.

I answer that the principalities of which one has record are found to be governed in two different ways; either by a prince, with a body of servants, who assist him to govern the kingdom as ministers by his favour and permission; or by a prince and barons, who hold that dignity by antiquity of blood and not by the grace of the prince. Such barons have states and their own subjects, who recognize them as lords and hold them in natural affection. Those states that are governed by a prince and his servants hold their prince in more consideration, because in all the country there is no one who is recognized as superior to him, and if they yield obedience to another they do it as to a minister and official, and they do not bear him any particular affection.

The examples of these two governments in our time are the Turk and the King of France. The entire monarchy of the Turk is governed by one lord, the others are his servants; and, dividing his kingdom into sanjaks, he sends there different administrators, and shifts and changes them as he chooses. But the King of France is placed in the midst of an ancient body of lords, acknowledged by their own subjects, and beloved by them; they have their own prerogatives, nor can the king take these away except at his peril. Therefore, he who considers both of these states will recognize great difficulties in seizing the state of the Turk, but, once it is conquered, great ease in holding it. The causes of the difficulties in seizing the kingdom of the Turk are that the usurper cannot be called in by the princes of the kingdom, nor can he hope to be assisted in his designs by the revolt of those whom the lord has around him. This arises from the reasons given above; for his ministers, being all slaves and bondmen, can only be corrupted with great difficulty, and one can expect little advantage from them when they have been corrupted, as they cannot carry the people with them, for the reasons assigned. Hence, he who attacks the Turk must bear in mind that he will find him united, and he will have to rely more on his own strength than on the revolt of others; but, if once the Turk has been conquered, and routed in the field in such a way that he cannot replace his armies, there is nothing to fear but the family of this prince, and, this being exterminated, there remains no one to fear, the others having no credit with the people; and as the conqueror did not rely on them before his victory, so he ought not to fear them after it.

The contrary happens in kingdoms governed like that of France, because one can easily enter there by gaining over some baron of the kingdom, for one always finds malcontents and such as desire a change. Such men, for the reasons given, can open the way into the state and render the victory easy; but if you wish to hold it afterwards, you meet with infinite difficulties, both from those who have assisted you and from those you have crushed. Nor is it enough for you to have exterminated the family of the prince, because the lords that remain make themselves the heads of fresh movements against you, and as you are unable either to satisfy or exterminate them, that state is lost whenever time brings the opportunity.

Now if you will consider what was the nature of the government of Darius, you will find it similar to the kingdom of the Turk, and therefore it was only necessary for Alexander, first to overthrow him in the field, and then to take the country from him. After which victory, Darius being killed, the state remained secure to Alexander, for the above reasons. And if his successors had been united they would have enjoyed it securely and at their ease, for there were no tumults raised in the kingdom except those they provoked themselves.

But it is impossible to hold with such tranquillity states constituted like that of France. Hence arose those frequent rebellions against the Romans in Spain, France, and Greece, owing to the many principalities there were in these states, of which, as long as the memory of them endured, the Romans always held an insecure possession; but with the power and long continuance of the empire the memory of them passed away, and the Romans then became secure possessors. And when fighting afterwards amongst themselves, each one was able to attach to himself his own parts of the country, according to the authority he had assumed there; and the family of the former lord being exterminated, none other than the Romans were acknowledged.

When these things are remembered no one will marvel at the ease with which Alexander held the Empire of Asia, or at the difficulties which others have had to keep an acquisition, such as Pyrrhus and many more; this is not occasioned by the little or abundance of ability in the conqueror, but by the want of uniformity in the subject state.

Chapter V
CONCERNING THE WAY TO GOVERN CITIES OR PRINCIPALITIES WHICH LIVED UNDER THEIR OWN LAWS BEFORE THEY WERE ANNEXED

Whenever those states which have been acquired as stated have been accustomed to live under their own laws and in freedom, there are three courses for those who wish to hold them: the first is to ruin them, the next is to reside there in person, the third is to permit them to live under their own laws, drawing a tribute, and establishing within it an oligarchy which will keep it friendly to you. Because such a government, being created by the prince, knows that it cannot stand without his friendship and interest, and does its utmost to support him; and therefore he who would keep a city accustomed to freedom will hold it more easily by the means of its own citizens than in any other way.

There are, for example, the Spartans and the Romans. The Spartans held Athens and Thebes, establishing there an oligarchy: nevertheless they lost them. The Romans, in order to hold Capua, Carthage, and Numantia, dismantled them, and did not lose them. They wished to hold Greece as the Spartans held it, making it free and permitting its laws, and did not succeed. So to hold it they were compelled to dismantle many cities in the country, for in truth there is no safe way to retain them otherwise than by ruining them. And he who becomes master of a city accustomed to freedom and does not destroy it, may expect to be destroyed by it, for in rebellion it has always the watchword of liberty and its ancient privileges as a rallying point, which neither time nor benefits will ever cause it to forget. And whatever you may do or provide against, they never forget that name or their privileges unless they are disunited or dispersed, but at every chance they immediately rally to them, as Pisa after the hundred years she had been held in bondage by the Florentines.

But when cities or countries are accustomed to live under a prince, and his family is exterminated, they, being on the one hand accustomed to obey and on the other hand not having the old prince, cannot agree in making one from amongst themselves, and they do not know how to govern themselves. For this reason they are very slow to take up arms, and a prince can gain them to himself and secure them much more easily. But in republics there is more vitality, greater hatred, and more desire for vengeance, which will never permit them to allow the memory of their former liberty to rest; so that the safest way is to destroy them or to reside there.

Chapter VI
CONCERNING NEW PRINCIPALITIES WHICH ARE ACQUIRED BY ONE'S OWN ARMS AND ABILITY

Let no one be surprised if, in speaking of entirely new principalities as I shall do, I adduce the highest examples both of prince and of state; because men, walking almost always in paths beaten by others, and following by imitation their deeds, are yet unable to keep entirely to the ways of others or attain to the power of those they imitate. A wise man ought always to follow the paths beaten by great men, and to imitate those who have been supreme, so that if his ability does not equal theirs, at least it will savour of it. Let him act like the clever archers who, designing to hit the mark which yet appears too far distant, and knowing the limits to which the strength of their bow attains, take aim much higher than the mark, not to reach by their strength or arrow to so great a height, but to be able with the aid of so high an aim to hit the mark they wish to reach.

I say, therefore, that in entirely new principalities, where there is a new prince, more or less difficulty is found in keeping them, accordingly as there is more or less ability in him who has acquired the state. Now, as the fact of becoming a prince from a private station presupposes either ability or fortune, it is clear that one or other of these things will mitigate in some degree many difficulties. Nevertheless, he who has relied least on fortune is established the strongest. Further, it facilitates matters when the prince, having no other state, is compelled to reside there in person.

But to come to those who, by their own ability and not through fortune, have risen to be princes, I say that Moses, Cyrus, Romulus, Theseus, and such like are the most excellent examples. And although one may not discuss Moses, he having been a mere executor of the will of God, yet he ought to be admired, if only for that favour which made him worthy to speak with God. But in considering Cyrus and others who have acquired or founded kingdoms, all will be found admirable; and if their particular deeds and conduct shall be considered, they will not be found inferior to those of Moses, although he had so great a preceptor. And in examining their actions and lives one cannot see that they owed anything to fortune beyond opportunity, which brought them the material to mould into the form which seemed best to them. Without that opportunity their powers of mind would have been extinguished, and without those powers the opportunity would have come in vain.

It was necessary, therefore, to Moses that he should find the people of Israel in Egypt enslaved and oppressed by the Egyptians, in order that they should be disposed to follow him so as to be delivered out of bondage. It was necessary that Romulus should not remain in Alba, and that he should be abandoned at his birth, in order that he should become King of Rome and founder of the fatherland. It was necessary that Cyrus should find the Persians discontented with the government of the Medes, and the Medes soft and effeminate through their long peace. Theseus could not have shown his ability had he not found the Athenians dispersed. These opportunities, therefore, made those men fortunate, and their high ability enabled them to recognize the opportunity whereby their country was ennobled and made famous.

Those who by valorous ways become princes, like these men, acquire a principality with difficulty, but they keep it with ease. The difficulties they have in acquiring it rise in part from the new rules and methods which they are forced to introduce to establish their government and its security. And it ought to be remembered that there is nothing more difficult to take in hand, more perilous to conduct, or more uncertain in its success, than to take the lead in the introduction of a new order of things, because the innovator has for enemies all those who have done well under the old conditions, and lukewarm defenders in those who may do well under the new. This coolness arises partly from fear of the opponents, who have the laws on their side, and partly from the incredulity of men, who do not readily believe in new things until they have had a long experience of them. Thus it happens that whenever those who are hostile have the opportunity to attack they do it like partisans, whilst the others defend lukewarmly, in such wise that the prince is endangered along with them.

It is necessary, therefore, if we desire to discuss this matter thoroughly, to inquire whether these innovators can rely on themselves or have to depend on others: that is to say, whether, to consummate their enterprise, have they to use prayers or can they use force? In the first instance they always succeed badly, and never compass anything; but when they can rely on themselves and use force, then they are rarely endangered. Hence it is that all armed prophets have conquered, and the unarmed ones have been destroyed. Besides the reasons mentioned, the nature of the people is variable, and whilst it is easy to persuade them, it is difficult to fix them in that persuasion. And thus it is necessary to take such measures that, when they believe no longer, it may be possible to make them believe by force.

If Moses, Cyrus, Theseus, and Romulus had been unarmed they could not have enforced their constitutions for long—as happened in our time to Fra Girolamo Savonarola, who was ruined with his new order of things immediately the multitude believed in him no longer, and he had no means of keeping steadfast those who believed or of making the unbelievers to believe. Therefore such as these have great difficulties in consummating their enterprise, for all their dangers are in the ascent, yet with ability they will overcome them; but when these are overcome, and those who envied them their success are exterminated, they will begin to be respected, and they will continue afterwards powerful, secure, honoured, and happy.

To these great examples I wish to add a lesser one; still it bears some resemblance to them, and I wish it to suffice me for all of a like kind: it is Hiero the Syracusan.[7] This man rose from a private station to be Prince of Syracuse, nor did he, either, owe anything to fortunc but opportunity; for the Syracusans, being oppressed, chose him for their captain, afterwards he was rewarded by being made their prince. He was of so great ability, even as a private citizen, that one who writes of him says he wanted nothing but a kingdom to be a king. This man abolished the old soldiery, organized the new, gave up old alliances, made new ones; and as he had his own soldiers and allies, on such foundations he was able to build any edifice: thus, whilst he had endured much trouble in acquiring, he had but little in keeping.

---

[7] Hiero II, born about 307 B.C., died 216 B.C.

Chapter VII
CONCERNING NEW PRINCIPALITIES WHICH ARE ACQUIRED EITHER BY THE ARMS OF OTHERS OR BY GOOD FORTUNE

Those who solely by good fortune become princes from being private citizens have little trouble in rising, but much in keeping atop; they have not any difficulties on the way up, because they fly, but they have many when they reach the summit. Such are those to whom some state is given either for money or by the favour of him who bestows it; as happened to many in Greece, in the cities of Ionia and of the Hellespont, where princes were made by Darius, in order that they might hold the cities both for his security and his glory; as also were those emperors who, by the corruption of the soldiers, from being citizens came to empire. Such stand simply elevated upon the goodwill and the fortune of him who has elevated them—two most inconstant and unstable things. Neither have they the knowledge requisite for the position; because, unless they are men of great worth and ability, it is not reasonable to expect that they should know how to command, having always lived in a private condition; besides, they cannot hold it because they have not forces which they can keep friendly and faithful.

States that rise unexpectedly, then, like all other things in nature which are born and grow rapidly, cannot leave their foundations and correspondencies[8] fixed in such a way that the first storm will not overthrow them; unless, as is said, those who unexpectedly become princes are men of so much ability that they know they have to be prepared at once to hold that which fortune has thrown into their laps, and that those foundations, which others have laid *before* they became princes, they must lay *afterwards*.

Concerning these two methods of rising to be a prince by ability or fortune, I wish to adduce two examples within our own recollection, and these are Francesco Sforza[9] and Cesare Borgia. Francesco, by proper means and with great ability, from being a private person rose to be Duke of Milan, and that which he had acquired with a thousand anxieties he kept with little trouble. On the other hand, Cesare Borgia, called by the people Duke Valentino, acquired his state during the ascendancy of his father, and on its decline he lost it, notwithstanding that he had taken every measure and done all that ought to be done by a wise and able man to fix firmly his roots in the states which the arms and fortunes of others had bestowed on him.

Because, as is stated above, he who has not first laid his foundations may be able with great ability to lay them afterwards, but they will be laid with trouble to the architect and danger to the building. If, therefore, all the steps taken by the duke be considered, it will be seen that he laid solid foundations for his future power, and I

---

8 "Le radici e corrispondenze," their roots (i.e. foundations) and correspondencies or relations with other states—a common meaning of "correspondence" and "correspondency" in the sixteenth and seventeenth centuries.

9 Francesco Sforza, born 1401, died 1466. He married Bianca Maria Visconti, a natural daughter of Filippo Visconti, the Duke of Milan, on whose death he procured his own elevation to the duchy. Machiavelli was the accredited agent of the Florentine Republic to Cesare Borgia (1478-1507) during the transactions which led up to the assassinations of the Orsini and Vitelli at Sinigalia, and along with his letters to his chiefs in Florence he has left an account, written ten years before *The Prince*, of the proceedings of the duke in his "Descritione del modo tenuto dal duca Valentino nello ammazzare Vitellozzo Vitelli," etc., a translation of which is appended to the present work.

do not consider it superfluous to discuss them, because I do not know what better precepts to give a new prince than the example of his actions; and if his dispositions were of no avail, that was not his fault, but the extraordinary and extreme malignity of fortune.

Alexander the Sixth, in wishing to aggrandize the duke, his son, had many immediate and prospective difficulties. Firstly, he did not see his way to make him master of any state that was not a state of the Church; and if he was willing to rob the Church he knew that the Duke of Milan and the Venetians would not consent, because Faenza and Rimini were already under the protection of the Venetians. Besides this, he saw the arms of Italy, especially those by which he might have been assisted, in hands that would fear the aggrandizement of the Pope, namely, the Orsini and the Colonnesi and their following. It behoved him, therefore, to upset this state of affairs and embroil the powers, so as to make himself securely master of part of their states. This was easy for him to do, because he found the Venetians, moved by other reasons, inclined to bring back the French into Italy; he would not only not oppose this, but he would render it more easy by dissolving the former marriage of King Louis. Therefore the king came into Italy with the assistance of the Venetians and the consent of Alexander. He was no sooner in Milan than the Pope had soldiers from him for the attempt on the Romagna, which yielded to him on the reputation of the king. The duke, therefore, having acquired the Romagna and beaten the Colonnesi, while wishing to hold that and to advance further, was hindered by two things: the one, his forces did not appear loyal to him, the other, the goodwill of France: that is to say, he feared that the forces of the Orsini, which he was using, would not stand to him, that not only might they hinder him from winning more, but might themselves seize what he had won, and that the king might also do the same. Of the Orsini he had a warning when, after taking Faenza and attacking Bologna, he saw them go very unwillingly to that attack. And as to the king, he learned his mind when he himself, after taking the Duchy of Urbino, attacked Tuscany, and the king made him desist from that undertaking; hence the duke decided to depend no more upon the arms and the luck of others.

For the first thing he weakened the Orsini and Colonnesi parties in Rome, by gaining to himself all their adherents who were gentlemen, making them his gentlemen, giving them good pay, and, according to their rank, honouring them with office and command in such a way that in a few months all attachment to the factions was destroyed and turned entirely to the duke. After this he awaited an opportunity to crush the Orsini, having scattered the adherents of the Colonna house. This came to him soon and he used it well; for the Orsini, perceiving at length that the aggrandizement of the duke and the Church was ruin to them, called a meeting of the Magione in Perugia. From this sprung the rebellion at Urbino and the tumults in the Romagna, with endless dangers to the duke, all of which he overcame with the help of the French. Having restored his authority, not to leave it at risk by trusting either to the French or other outside forces, he had recourse to his wiles, and he knew so well how to conceal his mind that, by the mediation of Signor Pagolo—whom the duke did not fail to secure with all kinds of attention, giving him money, apparel, and horses—the Orsini were reconciled, so that their simplicity brought them into his power at Sinigalia.[10] Having exterminated the leaders, and turned their partisans into his friends, the duke laid sufficiently good foundations to his power, having all the Romagna and the Duchy of Urbino; and the people now beginning to appreciate their prosperity, he gained them all over to himself. And as this point is worthy of notice, and to be imitated by others, I am not willing to leave it out.

When the duke occupied the Romagna he found it under the rule of weak masters, who rather plundered their subjects than ruled them, and gave them more cause for disunion than for union, so that the country was full of robbery, quarrels, and every kind of violence; and so, wishing to bring back peace and obedience to authority, he

[10] Sinigalia, 31st December 1502.

considered it necessary to give it a good governor. Thereupon he promoted Messer Ramiro d'Orco,[11] a swift and cruel man, to whom he gave the fullest power. This man in a short time restored peace and unity with the greatest success. Afterwards the duke considered that it was not advisable to confer such excessive authority, for he had no doubt but that he would become odious, so he set up a court of judgment in the country, under a most excellent president, wherein all cities had their advocates. And because he knew that the past severity had caused some hatred against himself, so, to clear himself in the minds of the people, and gain them entirely to himself, he desired to show that, if any cruelty had been practised, it had not originated with him, but in the natural sternness of the minister. Under this pretence he took Ramiro, and one morning caused him to be executed and left on the piazza at Cesena with the block and a bloody knife at his side. The barbarity of this spectacle caused the people to be at once satisfied and dismayed.

But let us return whence we started. I say that the duke, finding himself now sufficiently powerful and partly secured from immediate dangers by having armed himself in his own way, and having in a great measure crushed those forces in his vicinity that could injure him if he wished to proceed with his conquest, had next to consider France, for he knew that the king, who too late was aware of his mistake, would not support him. And from this time he began to seek new alliances and to temporize with France in the expedition which she was making towards the kingdom of Naples against the Spaniards who were besieging Gaeta. It was his intention to secure himself against them, and this he would have quickly accomplished had Alexander lived.

Such was his line of action as to present affairs. But as to the future he had to fear, in the first place, that a new successor to the Church might not be friendly to him and might seek to take from him that which Alexander had given him, so he decided to act in

---

[11] Ramiro d'Orco. Ramiro de Lorqua.

four ways. Firstly, by exterminating the families of those lords whom he had despoiled, so as to take away that pretext from the Pope. Secondly, by winning to himself all the gentlemen of Rome, so as to be able to curb the Pope with their aid, as has been observed. Thirdly, by converting the college more to himself. Fourthly, by acquiring so much power before the Pope should die that he could by his own measures resist the first shock. Of these four things, at the death of Alexander, he had accomplished three. For he had killed as many of the dispossessed lords as he could lay hands on, and few had escaped; he had won over the Roman gentlemen, and he had the most numerous party in the college. And as to any fresh acquisition, he intended to become master of Tuscany, for he already possessed Perugia and Piombino, and Pisa was under his protection. And as he had no longer to study France (for the French were already driven out of the kingdom of Naples by the Spaniards, and in this way both were compelled to buy his goodwill), he pounced down upon Pisa. After this, Lucca and Siena yielded at once, partly through hatred and partly through fear of the Florentines; and the Florentines would have had no remedy had he continued to prosper, as he was prospering the year that Alexander died, for he had acquired so much power and reputation that he would have stood by himself, and no longer have depended on the luck and the forces of others, but solely on his own power and ability.

But Alexander died five years after he had first drawn the sword. He left the duke with the state of Romagna alone consolidated, with the rest in the air, between two most powerful hostile armies, and sick unto death. Yet there were in the duke such boldness and ability, and he knew so well how men are to be won or lost, and so firm were the foundations which in so short a time he had laid, that if he had not had those armies on his back, or if he had been in good health, he would have overcome all difficulties. And it is seen that his foundations were good, for the Romagna awaited him for more than a month. In Rome, although but half alive, he remained secure; and whilst the Baglioni, the Vitelli, and the Orsini might come to

Rome, they could not effect anything against him. If he could not have made Pope him whom he wished, at least the one whom he did not wish would not have been elected. But if he had been in sound health at the death of Alexander,[12] everything would have been different to him. On the day that Julius the Second[13] was elected, he told me that he had thought of everything that might occur at the death of his father, and had provided a remedy for all, except that he had never anticipated that, when the death did happen, he himself would be on the point to die.

When all the actions of the duke are recalled, I do not know how to blame him, but rather it appears to be, as I have said, that I ought to offer him for imitation to all those who, by the fortune or the arms of others, are raised to government. Because he, having a lofty spirit and far-reaching aims, could not have regulated his conduct otherwise, and only the shortness of the life of Alexander and his own sickness frustrated his designs. Therefore, he who considers it necessary to secure himself in his new principality, to win friends, to overcome either by force or fraud, to make himself beloved and feared by the people, to be followed and revered by the soldiers, to exterminate those who have power or reason to hurt him, to change the old order of things for new, to be severe and gracious, magnanimous and liberal, to destroy a disloyal soldiery and to create new, to maintain friendship with kings and princes in such a way that they must help him with zeal and offend with caution, cannot find a more lively example than the actions of this man.

Only can he be blamed for the election of Julius the Second, in whom he made a bad choice, because, as is said, not being able to elect a Pope to his own mind, he could have hindered any other from being elected Pope; and he ought never to have consented to the election of any cardinal whom he had injured or who had cause

---

[12] Alexander VI died of fever, 18th August 1503.

[13] Julius II was Giuliano della Rovere, Cardinal of San Pietro ad Vincula, born 1443, died 1513.

to fear him if they became pontiffs. For men injure either from fear or hatred. Those whom he had injured, amongst others, were San Pietro ad Vincula, Colonna, San Giorgio, and Ascanio.[14] The rest, in becoming Pope, had to fear him, Rouen and the Spaniards excepted; the latter from their relationship and obligations, the former from his influence, the kingdom of France having relations with him. Therefore, above everything, the duke ought to have created a Spaniard Pope, and, failing him, he ought to have consented to Rouen and not San Pietro ad Vincula. He who believes that new benefits will cause great personages to forget old injuries is deceived. Therefore, the duke erred in his choice, and it was the cause of his ultimate ruin.

[14] San Giorgio is Raffaello Riario. Ascanio is Ascanio Sforza.

Chapter VIII
CONCERNING THOSE WHO HAVE OBTAINED A PRINCIPALITY BY WICKEDNESS

Although a prince may rise from a private station in two ways, neither of which can be entirely attributed to fortune or genius, yet it is manifest to me that I must not be silent on them, although one could be more copiously treated when I discuss republics. These methods are when, either by some wicked or nefarious ways, one ascends to the principality, or when by the favour of his fellow-citizens a private person becomes the prince of his country. And speaking of the first method, it will be illustrated by two examples—one ancient, the other modern—and without entering further into the subject, I consider these two examples will suffice those who may be compelled to follow them.

Agathocles, the Sicilian,[15] became King of Syracuse not only from a private but from a low and abject position. This man, the son of a potter, through all the changes in his fortunes always led an infamous life. Nevertheless, he accompanied his infamies with so much ability of mind and body that, having devoted himself to the military profession, he rose through its ranks to be Praetor of Syracuse. Being established in that position, and having deliberately resolved to make himself prince and to seize by violence, without obligation to others, that which had been conceded to him by assent, he came to an understanding for this purpose with Amilcar,

[15] Agathocles the Sicilian, born 361 B.C., died 289 B.C.

the Carthaginian, who, with his army, was fighting in Sicily. One morning he assembled the people and the senate of Syracuse, as if he had to discuss with them things relating to the Republic, and at a given signal the soldiers killed all the senators and the richest of the people; these dead, he seized and held the princedom of that city without any civil commotion. And although he was twice routed by the Carthaginians, and ultimately besieged, yet not only was he able to defend his city, but leaving part of his men for its defence, with the others he attacked Africa, and in a short time raised the siege of Syracuse. The Carthaginians, reduced to extreme necessity, were compelled to come to terms with Agathocles, and, leaving Sicily to him, had to be content with the possession of Africa.

Therefore, he who considers the actions and the genius of this man will see nothing, or little, which can be attributed to fortune, inasmuch as he attained pre-eminence, as is shown above, not by the favour of any one, but step by step in the military profession, which steps were gained with a thousand troubles and perils, and were afterwards boldly held by him with many hazardous dangers. Yet it cannot be called talent to slay fellow-citizens, to deceive friends, to be without faith, without mercy, without religion; such methods may gain empire, but not glory. Still, if the courage of Agathocles in entering into and extricating himself from dangers be considered, together with his greatness of mind in enduring and overcoming hardships, it cannot be seen why he should be esteemed less than the most notable captain. Nevertheless, his barbarous cruelty and inhumanity with infinite wickedness do not permit him to be celebrated among the most excellent men. What he achieved cannot be attributed either to fortune or genius.

In our times, during the rule of Alexander the Sixth, Oliverotto da Fermo, having been left an orphan many years before, was brought up by his maternal uncle, Giovanni Fogliani, and in the early days of his youth sent to fight under Pagolo Vitelli, that, being trained under his discipline, he might attain some high position in the military profession. After Pagolo died, he fought under his brother Vitellozzo, and in a very short time, being endowed with wit and a vigorous body and mind, he became the first man in his profession. But it appearing a paltry thing to serve under others, he resolved, with the aid of some citizens of Fermo, to whom the slavery of their country was dearer than its liberty, and with the help of the Vitelleschi, to seize Fermo. So he wrote to Giovanni Fogliani that, having been away from home for many years, he wished to visit him and his city, and in some measure to look upon his patrimony; and although he had not laboured to acquire anything except honour, yet, in order that the citizens should see he had not spent his time in vain, he desired to come honourably, so would be accompanied by one hundred horsemen, his friends and retainers; and he entreated Giovanni to arrange that he should be received honourably by the Fermians, all of which would be not only to his honour, but also to that of Giovanni himself, who had brought him up.

Giovanni, therefore, did not fail in any attentions due to his nephew, and he caused him to be honourably received by the Fermians, and he lodged him in his own house, where, having passed some days, and having arranged what was necessary for his wicked designs, Oliverotto gave a solemn banquet to which he invited Giovanni Fogliani and the chiefs of Fermo. When the viands and all the other entertainments that are usual in such banquets were finished, Oliverotto artfully began certain grave discourses, speaking of the greatness of Pope Alexander and his son Cesare, and of their enterprises, to which discourse Giovanni and others answered; but he rose at once, saying that such matters ought to be discussed in a more private place, and he betook himself to a chamber, whither Giovanni and the rest of the citizens went in after him. No sooner were they seated than soldiers issued from secret places and slaughtered Giovanni and the rest. After these murders Oliverotto, mounted on horseback, rode up and down the town and besieged the chief magistrate in the palace, so that in fear the people were forced to obey him, and to form a government, of which he made himself the prince. He killed all the malcontents who were able to injure him, and strengthened himself with new civil and military ordinances, in such a way that, in the year during which he held the principality, not only was he secure in the city of Fermo, but he had become formidable to all his neighbours. And his destruction would have been as difficult as that of Agathocles if he had not allowed himself to be overreached by Cesare Borgia, who took him with the Orsini and Vitelli at Sinigalia, as was stated above. Thus one year after he had committed this parricide, he was strangled, together with Vitellozzo, whom he had made his leader in valour and wickedness.

Some may wonder how it can happen that Agathocles, and his like, after infinite treacheries and cruelties, should live for long secure in his country, and defend himself from external enemies, and never be conspired against by his own citizens; seeing that many others, by means of cruelty, have never been able even in peaceful times to hold the state, still less in the doubtful times of war. I believe that this follows from severities[16] being badly or properly used. Those may be called properly used, if of evil it is possible to speak well, that are applied at one blow and are necessary to one's security, and that are not persisted in afterwards unless they can be turned to the advantage of the subjects. The badly employed are those which, notwithstanding they may be few in the commencement, multiply with time rather than decrease. Those who practise the first system are able, by aid of God or man, to mitigate in some degree their rule, as Agathocles did. It is impossible for those who follow the other to maintain themselves.

Hence it is to be remarked that, in seizing a state, the usurper ought to examine closely into all those injuries which it is necessary for him to inflict, and to do them all at one stroke so as not to have to repeat them daily; and thus by not unsettling men he will be able

---

[16] Mr Burd suggests that this word probably comes near the modern equivalent of Machiavelli's thought when he speaks of "crudelta" than the more obvious "cruelties."

to reassure them, and win them to himself by benefits. He who does otherwise, either from timidity or evil advice, is always compelled to keep the knife in his hand; neither can he rely on his subjects, nor can they attach themselves to him, owing to their continued and repeated wrongs. For injuries ought to be done all at one time, so that, being tasted less, they offend less; benefits ought to be given little by little, so that the flavour of them may last longer.

And above all things, a prince ought to live amongst his people in such a way that no unexpected circumstances, whether of good or evil, shall make him change; because if the necessity for this comes in troubled times, you are too late for harsh measures; and mild ones will not help you, for they will be considered as forced from you, and no one will be under any obligation to you for them.

Chapter IX
CONCERNING A CIVIL PRINCIPALITY

But coming to the other point—where a leading citizen becomes the prince of his country, not by wickedness or any intolerable violence, but by the favour of his fellow citizens—this may be called a civil principality: nor is genius or fortune altogether necessary to attain to it, but rather a happy shrewdness. I say then that such a principality is obtained either by the favour of the people or by the favour of the nobles. Because in all cities these two distinct parties are found, and from this it arises that the people do not wish to be ruled nor oppressed by the nobles, and the nobles wish to rule and oppress the people; and from these two opposite desires there arises in cities one of three results, either a principality, self-government, or anarchy.

A principality is created either by the people or by the nobles, accordingly as one or other of them has the opportunity; for the nobles, seeing they cannot withstand the people, begin to cry up the reputation of one of themselves, and they make him a prince, so that under his shadow they can give vent to their ambitions. The people, finding they cannot resist the nobles, also cry up the reputation of one of themselves, and make him a prince so as to be defended by his authority. He who obtains sovereignty by the assistance of the nobles maintains himself with more difficulty than he who comes to it by the aid of the people, because the former finds himself with many around him who consider themselves his equals, and because of this he can neither rule nor manage them to his liking. But he who reaches sovereignty by popular favour finds himself alone, and has none around him, or few, who are not prepared to obey him.

Besides this, one cannot by fair dealing, and without injury to others, satisfy the nobles, but you can satisfy the people, for their object is more righteous than that of the nobles, the latter wishing to oppress, while the former only desire not to be oppressed. It is to be added also that a prince can never secure himself against a hostile people, because of there being too many, whilst from the nobles he can secure himself, as they are few in number. The worst that a prince may expect from a hostile people is to be abandoned by them; but from hostile nobles he has not only to fear abandonment, but also that they will rise against him; for they, being in these affairs more far-seeing and astute, always come forward in time to save themselves, and to obtain favours from him whom they expect to prevail. Further, the prince is compelled to live always with the same people, but he can do well without the same nobles, being able to make and unmake them daily, and to give or take away authority when it pleases him.

Therefore, to make this point clearer, I say that the nobles ought to be looked at mainly in two ways: that is to say, they either shape their course in such a way as binds them entirely to your fortune, or they do not. Those who so bind themselves, and are not rapacious, ought to be honoured and loved; those who do not bind themselves may be dealt with in two ways; they may fail to do this through pusillanimity and a natural want of courage, in which case you ought to make use of them, especially of those who are of good counsel; and thus, whilst in prosperity you honour them, in adversity you do not have to fear them. But when for their own ambitious ends they shun binding themselves, it is a token that they are giving more thought to themselves than to you, and a prince ought to guard against such, and to fear them as if they were open enemies, because in adversity they always help to ruin him.

Therefore, one who becomes a prince through the favour of the people ought to keep them friendly, and this he can easily do seeing they only ask not to be oppressed by him. But one who, in opposition to the people, becomes a prince by the favour of the nobles, ought, above everything, to seek to win the people over to himself, and this he may easily do if he takes them under his protection. Because men, when they receive good from him of whom they were expecting evil, are bound more closely to their benefactor; thus the people quickly become more devoted to him than if he had been raised to the principality by their favours; and the prince can win their affections in many ways, but as these vary according to the circumstances one cannot give fixed rules, so I omit them; but, I repeat, it is necessary for a prince to have the people friendly, otherwise he has no security in adversity.

Nabis,[17] Prince of the Spartans, sustained the attack of all Greece, and of a victorious Roman army, and against them he defended his country and his government; and for the overcoming of this peril it was only necessary for him to make himself secure against a few, but this would not have been sufficient had the people been hostile. And do not let any one impugn this statement with the trite proverb that "He who builds on the people, builds on the mud," for this is true when a private citizen makes a foundation there, and persuades himself that the people will free him when he is oppressed by his enemies or by the magistrates; wherein he would find himself very often deceived, as happened to the Gracchi in Rome and to Messer Giorgio Scali[18] in Florence. But granted a prince who has established himself as above, who can command, and is a man of courage, undismayed in adversity, who does not fail in other qualifications, and who, by his resolution and energy, keeps the whole people encouraged—such a one will never find himself deceived in them, and it will be shown that he has laid his foundations well.

---

[17] Nabis, tyrant of Sparta, conquered by the Romans under Flamininus in 195 B.C.; killed 192 B.C.

[18] Messer Giorgio Scali. This event is to be found in Machiavelli's "Florentine History," Book III.

These principalities are liable to danger when they are passing from the civil to the absolute order of government, for such princes either rule personally or through magistrates. In the latter case their government is weaker and more insecure, because it rests entirely on the goodwill of those citizens who are raised to the magistracy, and who, especially in troubled times, can destroy the government with great ease, either by intrigue or open defiance; and the prince has not the chance amid tumults to exercise absolute authority, because the citizens and subjects, accustomed to receive orders from magistrates, are not of a mind to obey him amid these confusions, and there will always be in doubtful times a scarcity of men whom he can trust. For such a prince cannot rely upon what he observes in quiet times, when citizens have need of the state, because then every one agrees with him; they all promise, and when death is far distant they all wish to die for him; but in troubled times, when the state has need of its citizens, then he finds but few. And so much the more is this experiment dangerous, inasmuch as it can only be tried once. Therefore a wise prince ought to adopt such a course that his citizens will always in every sort and kind of circumstance have need of the state and of him, and then he will always find them faithful.

Chapter X

CONCERNING THE WAY IN WHICH THE STRENGTH OF ALL PRINCIPALITIES OUGHT TO BE MEASURED

It is necessary to consider another point in examining the character of these principalities: that is, whether a prince has such power that, in case of need, he can support himself with his own resources, or whether he has always need of the assistance of others. And to make this quite clear I say that I consider those who are able to support themselves by their own resources who can, either by abundance of men or money, raise a sufficient army to join battle against any one who comes to attack them; and I consider those always to have need of others who cannot show themselves against the enemy in the field, but are forced to defend themselves by sheltering behind walls. The first case has been discussed, but we will speak of it again should it recur. In the second case one can say nothing except to encourage such princes to provision and fortify their towns, and not on any account to defend the country. And whoever shall fortify his town well, and shall have managed the other concerns of his subjects in the way stated above, and to be often repeated, will never be attacked without great caution, for men are always adverse to enterprises where difficulties can be seen, and it will be seen not to be an easy thing to attack one who has his town well fortified, and is not hated by his people.

The cities of Germany are absolutely free, they own but little country around them, and they yield obedience to the emperor when it suits them, nor do they fear this or any other power they may have near them, because they are fortified in such a way that every one thinks the taking of them by assault would be tedious and difficult, seeing they have proper ditches and walls, they have sufficient artillery, and they always keep in public depots enough for one year's eating, drinking, and firing. And beyond this, to keep the people quiet and without loss to the state, they always have the means of giving work to the community in those labours that are the life and strength of the city, and on the pursuit of which the people are supported; they also hold military exercises in repute, and moreover have many ordinances to uphold them.

Therefore, a prince who has a strong city, and had not made himself odious, will not be attacked, or if any one should attack he will only be driven off with disgrace; again, because that the affairs of this world are so changeable, it is almost impossible to keep an army a whole year in the field without being interfered with. And whoever should reply: If the people have property outside the city, and see it burnt, they will not remain patient, and the long siege and self-interest will make them forget their prince; to this I answer that a powerful and courageous prince will overcome all such difficulties by giving at one time hope to his subjects that the evil will not be for long, at another time fear of the cruelty of the enemy, then preserving himself adroitly from those subjects who seem to him to be too bold.

Further, the enemy would naturally on his arrival at once burn and ruin the country at the time when the spirits of the people are still hot and ready for the defence; and, therefore, so much the less ought the prince to hesitate; because after a time, when spirits have cooled, the damage is already done, the ills are incurred, and there is no longer any remedy; and therefore they are so much the more ready to unite with their prince, he appearing to be under obligations to them now that their houses have been burnt and their possessions ruined in his defence. For it is the nature of men to be bound by the benefits they confer as much as by those they receive. Therefore, if everything is well considered, it will not be difficult for a wise prince to keep the minds of his citizens steadfast from first to last, when he does not fail to support and defend them.

Chapter XI
CONCERNING ECCLESIASTICAL PRINCIPALITIES

It only remains now to speak of ecclesiastical principalities, touching which all difficulties are prior to getting possession, because they are acquired either by capacity or good fortune, and they can be held without either; for they are sustained by the ancient ordinances of religion, which are so all-powerful, and of such a character that the principalities may be held no matter how their princes behave and live. These princes alone have states and do not defend them; and they have subjects and do not rule them; and the states, although unguarded, are not taken from them, and the subjects, although not ruled, do not care, and they have neither the desire nor the ability to alienate themselves. Such principalities only are secure and happy. But being upheld by powers, to which the human mind cannot reach, I shall speak no more of them, because, being exalted and maintained by God, it would be the act of a presumptuous and rash man to discuss them.

Nevertheless, if any one should ask of me how comes it that the Church has attained such greatness in temporal power, seeing that from Alexander backwards the Italian potentates (not only those who have been called potentates, but every baron and lord, though the smallest) have valued the temporal power very slightly—yet now a king of France trembles before it, and it has been able to drive him from Italy, and to ruin the Venetians—although this may be very manifest, it does not appear to me superfluous to recall it in some measure to memory.

Before Charles, King of France, passed into Italy,[19] this country was under the dominion of the Pope, the Venetians, the King of Naples, the Duke of Milan, and the Florentines. These potentates had two principal anxieties: the one, that no foreigner should enter Italy under arms; the other, that none of themselves should seize more territory. Those about whom there was the most anxiety were the Pope and the Venetians. To restrain the Venetians the union of all the others was necessary, as it was for the defence of Ferrara; and to keep down the Pope they made use of the barons of Rome, who, being divided into two factions, Orsini and Colonnesi, had always a pretext for disorder, and, standing with arms in their hands under the eyes of the Pontiff, kept the pontificate weak and powerless. And although there might arise sometimes a courageous pope, such as Sixtus, yet neither fortune nor wisdom could rid him of these annoyances. And the short life of a pope is also a cause of weakness; for in the ten years, which is the average life of a pope, he can with difficulty lower one of the factions; and if, so to speak, one people should almost destroy the Colonnesi, another would arise hostile to the Orsini, who would support their opponents, and yet would not have time to ruin the Orsini. This was the reason why the temporal powers of the pope were little esteemed in Italy.

Alexander the Sixth arose afterwards, who of all the pontiffs that have ever been showed how a pope with both money and arms was able to prevail; and through the instrumentality of the Duke Valentino, and by reason of the entry of the French, he brought about all those things which I have discussed above in the actions of the duke. And although his intention was not to aggrandize the Church, but the duke, nevertheless, what he did contributed to the greatness of the Church, which, after his death and the ruin of the duke, became the heir to all his labours.

Pope Julius came afterwards and found the Church strong, possessing all the Romagna, the barons of Rome reduced to impotence,

---

[19] Charles VIII invaded Italy in 1494.

and, through the chastisements of Alexander, the factions wiped out; he also found the way open to accumulate money in a manner such as had never been practised before Alexander's time. Such things Julius not only followed, but improved upon, and he intended to gain Bologna, to ruin the Venetians, and to drive the French out of Italy. All of these enterprises prospered with him, and so much the more to his credit, inasmuch as he did everything to strengthen the Church and not any private person. He kept also the Orsini and Colonnesi factions within the bounds in which he found them; and although there was among them some mind to make disturbance, nevertheless he held two things firm: the one, the greatness of the Church, with which he terrified them; and the other, not allowing them to have their own cardinals, who caused the disorders among them. For whenever these factions have their cardinals they do not remain quiet for long, because cardinals foster the factions in Rome and out of it, and the barons are compelled to support them, and thus from the ambitions of prelates arise disorders and tumults among the barons. For these reasons his Holiness Pope Leo[20] found the pontificate most powerful, and it is to be hoped that, if others made it great in arms, he will make it still greater and more venerated by his goodness and infinite other virtues.

[20] Pope Leo X was the Cardinal de' Medici.

Chapter XII
HOW MANY KINDS OF SOLDIERY THERE ARE, AND CONCERNING MERCENARIES

Having discoursed particularly on the characteristics of such principalities as in the beginning I proposed to discuss, and having considered in some degree the causes of there being good or bad, and having shown the methods by which many have sought to acquire them and to hold them, it now remains for me to discuss generally the means of offence and defence which belong to each of them.

We have seen above how necessary it is for a prince to have his foundations well laid, otherwise it follows of necessity he will go to ruin. The chief foundations of all states, new as well as old or composite, are good laws and good arms; and as there cannot be good laws where the state is not well armed, it follows that where they are well armed they have good laws. I shall leave the laws out of the discussion and shall speak of the arms.

I say, therefore, that the arms with which a prince defends his state are either his own, or they are mercenaries, auxiliaries, or mixed. Mercenaries and auxiliaries are useless and dangerous; and if one holds his state based on these arms, he will stand neither firm nor safe; for they are disunited, ambitious, and without discipline, unfaithful, valiant before friends, cowardly before enemies; they have neither the fear of God nor fidelity to men, and destruction is deferred only so long as the attack is; for in peace one is robbed by them, and in war by the enemy. The fact is, they have no other attraction or reason for keeping the field than a trifle of stipend, which is not sufficient to make them willing to die for you. They are ready enough to be your soldiers whilst you do not make war, but if war comes they take themselves off or run from the foe; which I should have little trouble to prove, for the ruin of Italy has been caused by nothing else than by resting all her hopes for many years on mercenaries, and although they formerly made some display and appeared valiant amongst themselves, yet when the foreigners came they showed what they were. Thus it was that Charles, King of France, was allowed to seize Italy with chalk in hand;[21] and he who told us that our sins were the cause of it told the truth, but they were not the sins he imagined, but those which I have related. And as they were the sins of princes, it is the princes who have also suffered the penalty.

I wish to demonstrate further the infelicity of these arms. The mercenary captains are either capable men or they are not; if they are, you cannot trust them, because they always aspire to their own greatness, either by oppressing you, who are their master, or others contrary to your intentions; but if the captain is not skilful, you are ruined in the usual way.

And if it be urged that whoever is armed will act in the same way, whether mercenary or not, I reply that when arms have to be resorted to, either by a prince or a republic, then the prince ought to go in person and perform the duty of a captain; the republic has to send its citizens, and when one is sent who does not turn out satisfactorily, it ought to recall him, and when one is worthy, to hold him by the laws so that he does not leave the command. And

---

[21] "With chalk in hand," "col gesso." This is one of the *bons mots* of Alexander VI, and refers to the ease with which Charles VIII seized Italy, implying that it was only necessary for him to send his quartermasters to chalk up the billets for his soldiers to conquer the country. *Cf.* "The History of Henry VII," by Lord Bacon: "King Charles had conquered the realm of Naples, and lost it again, in a kind of a felicity of a dream. He passed the whole length of Italy without resistance: so that it was true what Pope Alexander was wont to say: That the Frenchmen came into Italy with chalk in their hands, to mark up their lodgings, rather than with swords to fight."

experience has shown princes and republics, single-handed, making the greatest progress, and mercenaries doing nothing except damage; and it is more difficult to bring a republic, armed with its own arms, under the sway of one of its citizens than it is to bring one armed with foreign arms. Rome and Sparta stood for many ages armed and free. The Switzers are completely armed and quite free.

Of ancient mercenaries, for example, there are the Carthaginians, who were oppressed by their mercenary soldiers after the first war with the Romans, although the Carthaginians had their own citizens for captains. After the death of Epaminondas, Philip of Macedon was made captain of their soldiers by the Thebans, and after victory he took away their liberty.

Duke Filippo being dead, the Milanese enlisted Francesco Sforza against the Venetians, and he, having overcome the enemy at Caravaggio,[22] allied himself with them to crush the Milanese, his masters. His father, Sforza, having been engaged by Queen Johanna[23] of Naples, left her unprotected, so that she was forced to throw herself into the arms of the King of Aragon, in order to save her kingdom. And if the Venetians and Florentines formerly extended their dominions by these arms, and yet their captains did not make themselves princes, but have defended them, I reply that the Florentines in this case have been favoured by chance, for of the able captains, of whom they might have stood in fear, some have not conquered, some have been opposed, and others have turned their ambitions elsewhere. One who did not conquer was Giovanni Acuto,[24] and since he did not conquer his fidelity

---

[22] Battle of Caravaggio, 15th September 1448.

[23] Johanna II of Naples, the widow of Ladislao, King of Naples.

[24] Giovanni Acuto. An English knight whose name was Sir John Hawkwood. He fought in the English wars in France, and was knighted by Edward III; afterwards he collected a body of troops and went into Italy. These became the famous "White Company." He took part in many wars, and died in Florence in 1394. He was born about 1320 at Sible Hedingham, a village in Essex. He married Domnia, a daughter of Bernabo Visconti.

cannot be proved; but every one will acknowledge that, had he conquered, the Florentines would have stood at his discretion. Sforza had the Bracceschi always against him, so they watched each other. Francesco turned his ambition to Lombardy; Braccio against the Church and the kingdom of Naples. But let us come to that which happened a short while ago. The Florentines appointed as their captain Pagolo Vitelli, a most prudent man, who from a private position had risen to the greatest renown. If this man had taken Pisa, nobody can deny that it would have been proper for the Florentines to keep in with him, for if he became the soldier of their enemies they had no means of resisting, and if they held to him they must obey him. The Venetians, if their achievements are considered, will be seen to have acted safely and gloriously so long as they sent to war their own men, when with armed gentlemen and plebians they did valiantly. This was before they turned to enterprises on land, but when they began to fight on land they forsook this virtue and followed the custom of Italy. And in the beginning of their expansion on land, through not having much territory, and because of their great reputation, they had not much to fear from their captains; but when they expanded, as under Carmignuola,[25] they had a taste of this mistake; for, having found him a most valiant man (they beat the Duke of Milan under his leadership), and, on the other hand, knowing how lukewarm he was in the war, they feared they would no longer conquer under him, and for this reason they were not willing, nor were they able, to let him go; and so, not to lose again that which they had acquired, they were compelled, in order to secure themselves, to murder him. They had afterwards for their captains Bartolomeo da Bergamo, Roberto da San Severino, the count of Pitigliano,[26] and the like, under whom they had to dread loss and not

[25] Carmignuola. Francesco Bussone, born at Carmagnola about 1390, executed at Venice, 5th May 1432.

[26] Bartolomeo Colleoni of Bergamo; died 1457. Roberto of San Severino; died fighting for Venice against Sigismund, Duke of Austria, in 1487. "Primo capitano in Italia."—Machiavelli. Count of Pitigliano; Nicolo Orsini, born 1442, died 1510.

gain, as happened afterwards at Vaila,[27] where in one battle they lost that which in eight hundred years they had acquired with so much trouble. Because from such arms conquests come but slowly, long delayed and inconsiderable, but the losses sudden and portentous.

And as with these examples I have reached Italy, which has been ruled for many years by mercenaries, I wish to discuss them more seriously, in order that, having seen their rise and progress, one may be better prepared to counteract them. You must understand that the empire has recently come to be repudiated in Italy, that the Pope has acquired more temporal power, and that Italy has been divided up into more states, for the reason that many of the great cities took up arms against their nobles, who, formerly favoured by the emperor, were oppressing them, whilst the Church was favouring them so as to gain authority in temporal power: in many others their citizens became princes. From this it came to pass that Italy fell partly into the hands of the Church and of republics, and, the Church consisting of priests and the republic of citizens unaccustomed to arms, both commenced to enlist foreigners.

The first who gave renown to this soldiery was Alberigo da Conio,[28] the Romagnian. From the school of this man sprang, among others, Braccio and Sforza, who in their time were the arbiters of Italy. After these came all the other captains who till now have directed the arms of Italy; and the end of all their valour has been, that she has been overrun by Charles, robbed by Louis, ravaged by Ferdinand, and insulted by the Switzers. The principle that has guided them has been, first, to lower the credit of infantry so that they might increase their own. They did this because, subsisting on their pay and without territory, they were unable to support many soldiers, and a few infantry did not give them any authority; so they

[27] Battle of Vaila in 1509.

[28] Alberigo da Conio. Alberico da Barbiano, Count of Cunio in Romagna. He was the leader of the famous "Company of St George," composed entirely of Italian soldiers. He died in 1409.

were led to employ cavalry, with a moderate force of which they were maintained and honoured; and affairs were brought to such a pass that, in an army of twenty thousand soldiers, there were not to be found two thousand foot soldiers. They had, besides this, used every art to lessen fatigue and danger to themselves and their soldiers, not killing in the fray, but taking prisoners and liberating without ransom. They did not attack towns at night, nor did the garrisons of the towns attack encampments at night; they did not surround the camp either with stockade or ditch, nor did they campaign in the winter. All these things were permitted by their military rules, and devised by them to avoid, as I have said, both fatigue and dangers; thus they have brought Italy to slavery and contempt.

Chapter XIII
CONCERNING AUXILIARIES, MIXED SOLDIERY, AND ONE'S OWN

Auxiliaries, which are the other useless arm, are employed when a prince is called in with his forces to aid and defend, as was done by Pope Julius in the most recent times; for he, having, in the enterprise against Ferrara, had poor proof of his mercenaries, turned to auxiliaries, and stipulated with Ferdinand, King of Spain,[29] for his assistance with men and arms. These arms may be useful and good in themselves, but for him who calls them in they are always disadvantageous; for losing, one is undone, and winning, one is their captive.

And although ancient histories may be full of examples, I do not wish to leave this recent one of Pope Julius the Second, the peril of which cannot fail to be perceived; for he, wishing to get Ferrara, threw himself entirely into the hands of the foreigner. But his good fortune brought about a third event, so that he did not reap the fruit of his rash choice; because, having his auxiliaries routed at Ravenna, and the Switzers having risen and driven out the conquerors (against all expectation, both his and others), it so came to pass that he did not become prisoner to his enemies, they having fled, nor to his auxiliaries, he having conquered by other arms than theirs.

The Florentines, being entirely without arms, sent ten thousand Frenchmen to take Pisa, whereby they ran more danger than at any

---

[29] Ferdinand V (F. II of Aragon and Sicily, F. III of Naples), surnamed "The Catholic," born 1452, died 1516.

other time of their troubles.

The Emperor of Constantinople,[30] to oppose his neighbours, sent ten thousand Turks into Greece, who, on the war being finished, were not willing to quit; this was the beginning of the servitude of Greece to the infidels.

Therefore, let him who has no desire to conquer make use of these arms, for they are much more hazardous than mercenaries, because with them the ruin is ready made; they are all united, all yield obedience to others; but with mercenaries, when they have conquered, more time and better opportunities are needed to injure you; they are not all of one community, they are found and paid by you, and a third party, which you have made their head, is not able all at once to assume enough authority to injure you. In conclusion, in mercenaries dastardy is most dangerous; in auxiliaries, valour. The wise prince, therefore, has always avoided these arms and turned to his own; and has been willing rather to lose with them than to conquer with the others, not deeming that a real victory which is gained with the arms of others.

I shall never hesitate to cite Cesare Borgia and his actions. This duke entered the Romagna with auxiliaries, taking there only French soldiers, and with them he captured Imola and Forli; but afterwards, such forces not appearing to him reliable, he turned to mercenaries, discerning less danger in them, and enlisted the Orsini and Vitelli; whom presently, on handling and finding them doubtful, unfaithful, and dangerous, he destroyed and turned to his own men. And the difference between one and the other of these forces can easily be seen when one considers the difference there was in the reputation of the duke, when he had the French, when he had the Orsini and Vitelli, and when he relied on his own soldiers, on whose fidelity he could always count and found it ever increasing; he was never esteemed more highly than when every one saw that he was complete master of his own forces.

---

[30] Joannes Cantacuzenus, born 1300, died 1383.

I was not intending to go beyond Italian and recent examples, but I am unwilling to leave out Hiero, the Syracusan, he being one of those I have named above. This man, as I have said, made head of the army by the Syracusans, soon found out that a mercenary soldiery, constituted like our Italian condottieri, was of no use; and it appearing to him that he could neither keep them nor let them go, he had them all cut to pieces, and afterwards made war with his own forces and not with aliens.

I wish also to recall to memory an instance from the Old Testament applicable to this subject. David offered himself to Saul to fight with Goliath, the Philistine champion, and, to give him courage, Saul armed him with his own weapons; which David rejected as soon as he had them on his back, saying he could make no use of them, and that he wished to meet the enemy with his sling and his knife. In conclusion, the arms of others either fall from your back, or they weigh you down, or they bind you fast.

Charles the Seventh,[31] the father of King Louis the Eleventh,[32] having by good fortune and valour liberated France from the English, recognized the necessity of being armed with forces of his own, and he established in his kingdom ordinances concerning men-at-arms and infantry. Afterwards his son, King Louis, abolished the infantry and began to enlist the Switzers, which mistake, followed by others, is, as is now seen, a source of peril to that kingdom; because, having raised the reputation of the Switzers, he has entirely diminished the value of his own arms, for he has destroyed the infantry altogether; and his men-at-arms he has subordinated to others, for, being as they are so accustomed to fight along with Switzers, it does not appear that they can now conquer without them. Hence it arises that the French cannot stand against the Switzers, and without the Switzers they do not come off well against others. The armies of the French have thus become mixed, partly mercenary and partly

[31] Charles VII of France, surnamed "The Victorious," born 1403, died 1461.
[32] Louis XI, son of the above, born 1423, died 1483.

national, both of which arms together are much better than mercenaries alone or auxiliaries alone, but much inferior to one's own forces. And this example proves it, for the kingdom of France would be unconquerable if the ordinance of Charles had been enlarged or maintained.

But the scanty wisdom of man, on entering into an affair which looks well at first, cannot discern the poison that is hidden in it, as I have said above of hectic fevers. Therefore, if he who rules a principality cannot recognize evils until they are upon him, he is not truly wise; and this insight is given to few. And if the first disaster to the Roman Empire[33] should be examined, it will be found to have commenced only with the enlisting of the Goths; because from that time the vigour of the Roman Empire began to decline, and all that valour which had raised it passed away to others.

I conclude, therefore, that no principality is secure without having its own forces; on the contrary, it is entirely dependent on good fortune, not having the valour which in adversity would defend it. And it has always been the opinion and judgment of wise men that nothing can be so uncertain or unstable as fame or power not founded on its own strength. And one's own forces are those which are composed either of subjects, citizens, or dependents; all others are mercenaries or auxiliaries. And the way to make ready one's own forces will be easily found if the rules suggested by me shall be reflected upon, and if one will consider how Philip, the father of Alexander the Great, and many republics and princes have armed and organized themselves, to which rules I entirely commit myself.

---

[33] "Many speakers to the House the other night in the debate on the reduction of armaments seemed to show a most lamentable ignorance of the conditions under which the British Empire maintains its existence. When Mr Balfour replied to the allegations that the Roman Empire sank under the weight of its military obligations, he said that this was 'wholly unhistorical.' He might well have added that the Roman power was at its zenith when every citizen acknowledged his liability to fight for the State, but that it began to decline as soon as this obligation was no longer recognised."—*Pall Mall Gazette*, 15th May 1906.

Chapter XIV
THAT WHICH CONCERNS A PRINCE ON THE SUBJECT OF THE ART OF WAR

A prince ought to have no other aim or thought, nor select anything else for his study, than war and its rules and discipline; for this is the sole art that belongs to him who rules, and it is of such force that it not only upholds those who are born princes, but it often enables men to rise from a private station to that rank. And, on the contrary, it is seen that when princes have thought more of ease than of arms they have lost their states. And the first cause of your losing it is to neglect this art; and what enables you to acquire a state is to be master of the art. Francesco Sforza, through being martial, from a private person became Duke of Milan; and the sons, through avoiding the hardships and troubles of arms, from dukes became private persons. For among other evils which being unarmed brings you, it causes you to be despised, and this is one of those ignominies against which a prince ought to guard himself, as is shown later on. Because there is nothing proportionate between the armed and the unarmed; and it is not reasonable that he who is armed should yield obedience willingly to him who is unarmed, or that the unarmed man should be secure among armed servants. Because, there being in the one disdain and in the other suspicion, it is not possible for them to work well together. And therefore a prince who does not understand the art of war, over and above the other misfortunes already mentioned, cannot be respected by his soldiers, nor can he rely on them. He ought never, therefore, to have out of his thoughts this subject of war, and in peace he should addict himself more to its exercise than in war; this he can do in two ways, the one by action, the other by study.

As regards action, he ought above all things to keep his men well organized and drilled, to follow incessantly the chase, by which he accustoms his body to hardships, and learns something of the nature of localities, and gets to find out how the mountains rise, how the valleys open out, how the plains lie, and to understand the nature of rivers and marshes, and in all this to take the greatest care. Which knowledge is useful in two ways. Firstly, he learns to know his country, and is better able to undertake its defence; afterwards, by means of the knowledge and observation of that locality, he understands with ease any other which it may be necessary for him to study hereafter; because the hills, valleys, and plains, and rivers and marshes that are, for instance, in Tuscany, have a certain resemblance to those of other countries, so that with a knowledge of the aspect of one country one can easily arrive at a knowledge of others. And the prince that lacks this skill lacks the essential which it is desirable that a captain should possess, for it teaches him to surprise his enemy, to select quarters, to lead armies, to array the battle, to besiege towns to advantage.

Philopoemen,[34] Prince of the Achaeans, among other praises which writers have bestowed on him, is commended because in time of peace he never had anything in his mind but the rules of war; and when he was in the country with friends, he often stopped and reasoned with them: "If the enemy should be upon that hill, and we should find ourselves here with our army, with whom would be the advantage? How should one best advance to meet him, keeping the ranks? If we should wish to retreat, how ought we to pursue?" And he would set forth to them, as he went, all the chances that could befall an army; he would listen to their opinion and state his,

---

[34] Philopoemen, "the last of the Greeks," born 252 B.C., died 183 B.C.

confirming it with reasons, so that by these continual discussions there could never arise, in time of war, any unexpected circumstances that he could not deal with.

But to exercise the intellect the prince should read histories, and study there the actions of illustrious men, to see how they have borne themselves in war, to examine the causes of their victories and defeat, so as to avoid the latter and imitate the former; and above all do as an illustrious man did, who took as an exemplar one who had been praised and famous before him, and whose achievements and deeds he always kept in his mind, as it is said Alexander the Great imitated Achilles, Caesar Alexander, Scipio Cyrus. And whoever reads the life of Cyrus, written by Xenophon, will recognize afterwards in the life of Scipio how that imitation was his glory, and how in chastity, affability, humanity, and liberality Scipio conformed to those things which have been written of Cyrus by Xenophon. A wise prince ought to observe some such rules, and never in peaceful times stand idle, but increase his resources with industry in such a way that they may be available to him in adversity, so that if fortune chances it may find him prepared to resist her blows.

Chapter XV
CONCERNING THINGS FOR WHICH MEN, AND ESPECIALLY PRINCES, ARE PRAISED OR BLAMED

It remains now to see what ought to be the rules of conduct for a prince towards subject and friends. And as I know that many have written on this point, I expect I shall be considered presumptuous in mentioning it again, especially as in discussing it I shall depart from the methods of other people. But, it being my intention to write a thing which shall be useful to him who apprehends it, it appears to me more appropriate to follow up the real truth of the matter than the imagination of it; for many have pictured republics and principalities which in fact have never been known or seen, because how one lives is so far distant from how one ought to live, that he who neglects what is done for what ought to be done, sooner effects his ruin than his preservation; for a man who wishes to act entirely up to his professions of virtue soon meets with what destroys him among so much that is evil.

Hence it is necessary for a prince wishing to hold his own to know how to do wrong, and to make use of it or not according to necessity. Therefore, putting on one side imaginary things concerning a prince, and discussing those which are real, I say that all men when they are spoken of, and chiefly princes for being more highly placed, are remarkable for some of those qualities which bring them either blame or praise; and thus it is that one is reputed liberal, another miserly, using a Tuscan term (because an avaricious person in our language is still he who desires to possess by robbery, whilst we call one miserly who deprives himself too much of the use of his own); one is reputed generous, one rapacious; one cruel, one compassionate; one faithless, another faithful; one effeminate and cowardly, another bold and brave; one affable, another haughty; one lascivious, another chaste; one sincere, another cunning; one hard, another easy; one grave, another frivolous; one religious, another unbelieving, and the like. And I know that every one will confess that it would be most praiseworthy in a prince to exhibit all the above qualities that are considered good; but because they can neither be entirely possessed nor observed, for human conditions do not permit it, it is necessary for him to be sufficiently prudent that he may know how to avoid the reproach of those vices which would lose him his state; and also to keep himself, if it be possible, from those which would not lose him it; but this not being possible, he may with less hesitation abandon himself to them. And again, he need not make himself uneasy at incurring a reproach for those vices without which the state can only be saved with difficulty, for if everything is considered carefully, it will be found that something which looks like virtue, if followed, would be his ruin; whilst something else, which looks like vice, yet followed brings him security and prosperity.

Chapter XVI
CONCERNING LIBERALITY AND MEANNESS

Commencing then with the first of the above-named characteristics, I say that it would be well to be reputed liberal. Nevertheless, liberality exercised in a way that does not bring you the reputation for it, injures you; for if one exercises it honestly and as it should be exercised, it may not become known, and you will not avoid the reproach of its opposite. Therefore, any one wishing to maintain among men the name of liberal is obliged to avoid no attribute of magnificence; so that a prince thus inclined will consume in such acts all his property, and will be compelled in the end, if he wish to maintain the name of liberal, to unduly weigh down his people, and tax them, and do everything he can to get money. This will soon make him odious to his subjects, and becoming poor he will be little valued by any one; thus, with his liberality, having offended many and rewarded few, he is affected by the very first trouble and imperilled by whatever may be the first danger; recognizing this himself, and wishing to draw back from it, he runs at once into the reproach of being miserly.

Therefore, a prince, not being able to exercise this virtue of liberality in such a way that it is recognized, except to his cost, if he is wise he ought not to fear the reputation of being mean, for in time he will come to be more considered than if liberal, seeing that with his economy his revenues are enough, that he can defend himself against all attacks, and is able to engage in enterprises without burdening his people; thus it comes to pass that he exercises liberality towards all from whom he does not take, who are numberless, and meanness towards those to whom he does not give, who are few.

We have not seen great things done in our time except by those who have been considered mean; the rest have failed. Pope Julius the Second was assisted in reaching the papacy by a reputation for liberality, yet he did not strive afterwards to keep it up, when he made war on the King of France; and he made many wars without imposing any extraordinary tax on his subjects, for he supplied his additional expenses out of his long thriftiness. The present King of Spain would not have undertaken or conquered in so many enterprises if he had been reputed liberal. A prince, therefore, provided that he has not to rob his subjects, that he can defend himself, that he does not become poor and abject, that he is not forced to become rapacious, ought to hold of little account a reputation for being mean, for it is one of those vices which will enable him to govern.

And if any one should say: Caesar obtained empire by liberality, and many others have reached the highest positions by having been liberal, and by being considered so, I answer: Either you are a prince in fact, or in a way to become one. In the first case this liberality is dangerous, in the second it is very necessary to be considered liberal; and Caesar was one of those who wished to become pre-eminent in Rome; but if he had survived after becoming so, and had not moderated his expenses, he would have destroyed his government. And if any one should reply: Many have been princes, and have done great things with armies, who have been considered very liberal, I reply: Either a prince spends that which is his own or his subjects' or else that of others. In the first case he ought to be sparing, in the second he ought not to neglect any opportunity for liberality. And to the prince who goes forth with his army, supporting it by pillage, sack, and extortion, handling that which belongs to others, this liberality is necessary, otherwise he would not be followed by soldiers. And of that which is neither yours nor your subjects' you can be a ready giver, as were Cyrus, Caesar, and Alexander; because it does not take away your reputation if you squander that of others, but adds to it; it is only squandering your own that injures you.

And there is nothing wastes so rapidly as liberality, for even whilst you exercise it you lose the power to do so, and so become either poor or despised, or else, in avoiding poverty, rapacious and hated. And a prince should guard himself, above all things, against being despised and hated; and liberality leads you to both. Therefore it is wiser to have a reputation for meanness which brings reproach without hatred, than to be compelled through seeking a reputation for liberality to incur a name for rapacity which begets reproach with hatred.

Chapter XVII
CONCERNING CRUELTY AND CLEMENCY, AND WHETHER IT IS BETTER TO BE LOVED THAN FEARED

Coming now to the other qualities mentioned above, I say that every prince ought to desire to be considered clement and not cruel. Nevertheless he ought to take care not to misuse this clemency. Cesare Borgia was considered cruel; notwithstanding, his cruelty reconciled the Romagna, unified it, and restored it to peace and loyalty. And if this be rightly considered, he will be seen to have been much more merciful than the Florentine people, who, to avoid a reputation for cruelty, permitted Pistoia to be destroyed.[35] Therefore a prince, so long as he keeps his subjects united and loyal, ought not to mind the reproach of cruelty; because with a few examples he will be more merciful than those who, through too much mercy, allow disorders to arise, from which follow murders or robberies; for these are wont to injure the whole people, whilst those executions which originate with a prince offend the individual only.

And of all princes, it is impossible for the new prince to avoid the imputation of cruelty, owing to new states being full of dangers. Hence Virgil, through the mouth of Dido, excuses the inhumanity of her reign owing to its being new, saying:

---

[35] During the rioting between the Cancellieri and Panciatichi factions in 1502 and 1503.

"Res dura, et regni novitas me talia cogunt
Moliri, et late fines custode tueri."[36]

Nevertheless he ought to be slow to believe and to act, nor should he himself show fear, but proceed in a temperate manner with prudence and humanity, so that too much confidence may not make him incautious and too much distrust render him intolerable.

Upon this a question arises: whether it be better to be loved than feared or feared than loved? It may be answered that one should wish to be both, but, because it is difficult to unite them in one person, it is much safer to be feared than loved, when, of the two, either must be dispensed with. Because this is to be asserted in general of men, that they are ungrateful, fickle, false, cowardly, covetous, and as long as you succeed they are yours entirely; they will offer you their blood, property, life, and children, as is said above, when the need is far distant; but when it approaches they turn against you. And that prince who, relying entirely on their promises, has neglected other precautions, is ruined; because friendships that are obtained by payments, and not by greatness or nobility of mind, may indeed be earned, but they are not secured, and in time of need cannot be relied upon; and men have less scruple in offending one who is beloved than one who is feared, for love is preserved by the link of obligation which, owing to the baseness of men, is broken at every opportunity for their advantage; but fear preserves you by a dread of punishment which never fails.

Nevertheless a prince ought to inspire fear in such a way that, if he does not win love, he avoids hatred; because he can endure very well being feared whilst he is not hated, which will always be

---

[36] … against my will, my fate
A throne unsettled, and an infant state,
Bid me defend my realms with all my pow'rs,
And guard with these severities my shores.

Christopher Pitt.

as long as he abstains from the property of his citizens and subjects and from their women. But when it is necessary for him to proceed against the life of someone, he must do it on proper justification and for manifest cause, but above all things he must keep his hands off the property of others, because men more quickly forget the death of their father than the loss of their patrimony. Besides, pretexts for taking away the property are never wanting; for he who has once begun to live by robbery will always find pretexts for seizing what belongs to others; but reasons for taking life, on the contrary, are more difficult to find and sooner lapse. But when a prince is with his army, and has under control a multitude of soldiers, then it is quite necessary for him to disregard the reputation of cruelty, for without it he would never hold his army united or disposed to its duties.

Among the wonderful deeds of Hannibal this one is enumerated: that having led an enormous army, composed of many various races of men, to fight in foreign lands, no dissensions arose either among them or against the prince, whether in his bad or in his good fortune. This arose from nothing else than his inhuman cruelty, which, with his boundless valour, made him revered and terrible in the sight of his soldiers, but without that cruelty, his other virtues were not sufficient to produce this effect. And short-sighted writers admire his deeds from one point of view and from another condemn the principal cause of them. That it is true his other virtues would not have been sufficient for him may be proved by the case of Scipio, that most excellent man, not only of his own times but within the memory of man, against whom, nevertheless, his army rebelled in Spain; this arose from nothing but his too great forbearance, which gave his soldiers more license than is consistent with military discipline. For this he was upbraided in the Senate by Fabius Maximus, and called the corrupter of the Roman soldiery. The Locrians were laid waste by a legate of Scipio, yet they were not avenged by him, nor was the insolence of the legate punished, owing entirely to his easy nature. Insomuch that someone in the Senate, wishing to excuse him, said there were many men who knew much better how not to err than to correct the errors of others. This disposition, if he had been continued in the command, would have destroyed in time the fame and glory of Scipio; but, he being under the control of the Senate, this injurious characteristic not only concealed itself, but contributed to his glory.

Returning to the question of being feared or loved, I come to the conclusion that, men loving according to their own will and fearing according to that of the prince, a wise prince should establish himself on that which is in his own control and not in that of others; he must endeavour only to avoid hatred, as is noted.

Chapter XVIII[37]
CONCERNING THE WAY IN WHICH PRINCES SHOULD KEEP FAITH

Every one admits how praiseworthy it is in a prince to keep faith, and to live with integrity and not with craft. Nevertheless our experience has been that those princes who have done great things have held good faith of little account, and have known how to circumvent the intellect of men by craft, and in the end have overcome those who have relied on their word. You must know there are two ways of contesting,[38] the one by the law, the other by force; the first method is proper to men, the second to beasts; but because the first is frequently not sufficient, it is necessary to have recourse to the second. Therefore it is necessary for a prince to understand how to avail himself of the beast and the man. This has been figuratively taught to princes by ancient writers, who describe how Achilles and many other princes of old were given to the Centaur Chiron to nurse, who brought them up in his discipline; which means solely that, as they had for a teacher one who was half beast and half man, so it is necessary for a prince to know how to make use of both natures,

---

37 "The present chapter has given greater offence than any other portion of Machiavelli's writings." Burd, "Il Principe," p. 297.

38 "Contesting," *i.e.* "striving for mastery." Mr Burd points out that this passage is imitated directly from Cicero's "De Officiis": "Nam cum sint duo genera decertandi, unum per disceptationem, alterum per vim; cumque illud proprium sit hominis, hoc beluarum; confugiendum est ad posterius, si uti non licet superiore."

and that one without the other is not durable. A prince, therefore, being compelled knowingly to adopt the beast, ought to choose the fox and the lion; because the lion cannot defend himself against snares and the fox cannot defend himself against wolves. Therefore, it is necessary to be a fox to discover the snares and a lion to terrify the wolves. Those who rely simply on the lion do not understand what they are about. Therefore a wise lord cannot, nor ought he to, keep faith when such observance may be turned against him, and when the reasons that caused him to pledge it exist no longer. If men were entirely good this precept would not hold, but because they are bad, and will not keep faith with you, you too are not bound to observe it with them. Nor will there ever be wanting to a prince legitimate reasons to excuse this non-observance. Of this endless modern examples could be given, showing how many treaties and engagements have been made void and of no effect through the faithlessness of princes; and he who has known best how to employ the fox has succeeded best.

But it is necessary to know well how to disguise this characteristic, and to be a great pretender and dissembler; and men are so simple, and so subject to present necessities, that he who seeks to deceive will always find someone who will allow himself to be deceived. One recent example I cannot pass over in silence. Alexander the Sixth did nothing else but deceive men, nor ever thought of doing otherwise, and he always found victims; for there never was a man who had greater power in asserting, or who with greater oaths would affirm a thing, yet would observe it less; nevertheless his deceits always succeeded according to his wishes,[39] because he well understood this side of mankind.

---

[39] "Nondimanco sempre gli succederono gli inganni (ad votum)." The words "ad votum" are omitted in the Testina addition, 1550.

Alexander never did what he said,
Cesare never said what he did.

Italian Proverb.

Therefore it is unnecessary for a prince to have all the good qualities I have enumerated, but it is very necessary to appear to have them. And I shall dare to say this also, that to have them and always to observe them is injurious, and that to appear to have them is useful; to appear merciful, faithful, humane, religious, upright, and to be so, but with a mind so framed that should you require not to be so, you may be able and know how to change to the opposite.

And you have to understand this, that a prince, especially a new one, cannot observe all those things for which men are esteemed, being often forced, in order to maintain the state, to act contrary to fidelity,[40] friendship, humanity, and religion. Therefore it is necessary for him to have a mind ready to turn itself accordingly as the winds and variations of fortune force it, yet, as I have said above, not to diverge from the good if he can avoid doing so, but, if compelled, then to know how to set about it.

For this reason a prince ought to take care that he never lets anything slip from his lips that is not replete with the above-named five qualities, that he may appear to him who sees and hears him altogether merciful, faithful, humane, upright, and religious. There is nothing more necessary to appear to have than this last quality, inasmuch as men judge generally more by the eye than by the hand, because it belongs to everybody to see you, to few to come in touch with you. Every one sees what you appear to be, few really know

---

[40] "Contrary to fidelity" or "faith," "contro alla fede," and "tutto fede," "altogether faithful," in the next paragraph. It is noteworthy that these two phrases, "contro alla fede" and "tutto fede," were omitted in the Testina edition, which was published with the sanction of the papal authorities. It may be that the meaning attached to the word "fede" was "the faith," *i.e.* the Catholic creed, and not as rendered here "fidelity" and "faithful." Observe that the word "religione" was suffered to stand in the text of the Testina, being used to signify indifferently every shade of belief, as witness "the religion," a phrase inevitably employed to designate the Huguenot heresy. South in his Sermon IX, p. 69, ed. 1843, comments on this passage as follows: "That great patron and Coryphaeus of this tribe, Nicolo Machiavel, laid down this for a master rule in his political scheme: 'That the show of religion was helpful to the politician, but the reality of it hurtful and pernicious.'"

what you are, and those few dare not oppose themselves to the opinion of the many, who have the majesty of the state to defend them; and in the actions of all men, and especially of princes, which it is not prudent to challenge, one judges by the result.

For that reason, let a prince have the credit of conquering and holding his state, the means will always be considered honest, and he will be praised by everybody; because the vulgar are always taken by what a thing seems to be and by what comes of it; and in the world there are only the vulgar, for the few find a place there only when the many have no ground to rest on.

One prince[41] of the present time, whom it is not well to name, never preaches anything else but peace and good faith, and to both he is most hostile, and either, if he had kept it, would have deprived him of reputation and kingdom many a time.

---

[41] Ferdinand of Aragon. "When Machiavelli was writing *The Prince* it would have been clearly impossible to mention Ferdinand's name here without giving offence." Burd's "Il Principe," p. 308.

Chapter XIX

THAT ONE SHOULD AVOID BEING DESPISED AND HATED

Now, concerning the characteristics of which mention is made above, I have spoken of the more important ones, the others I wish to discuss briefly under this generality, that the prince must consider, as has been in part said before, how to avoid those things which will make him hated or contemptible; and as often as he shall have succeeded he will have fulfilled his part, and he need not fear any danger in other reproaches.

It makes him hated above all things, as I have said, to be rapacious, and to be a violator of the property and women of his subjects, from both of which he must abstain. And when neither their property nor their honor is touched, the majority of men live content, and he has only to contend with the ambition of a few, whom he can curb with ease in many ways.

It makes him contemptible to be considered fickle, frivolous, effeminate, mean-spirited, irresolute, from all of which a prince should guard himself as from a rock; and he should endeavour to show in his actions greatness, courage, gravity, and fortitude; and in his private dealings with his subjects let him show that his judgments are irrevocable, and maintain himself in such reputation that no one can hope either to deceive him or to get round him.

That prince is highly esteemed who conveys this impression of himself, and he who is highly esteemed is not easily conspired against; for, provided it is well known that he is an excellent man and revered by his people, he can only be attacked with difficulty.

For this reason a prince ought to have two fears, one from within, on account of his subjects, the other from without, on account of external powers. From the latter he is defended by being well armed and having good allies, and if he is well armed he will have good friends, and affairs will always remain quiet within when they are quiet without, unless they should have been already disturbed by conspiracy; and even should affairs outside be disturbed, if he has carried out his preparations and has lived as I have said, as long as he does not despair, he will resist every attack, as I said Nabis the Spartan did.

But concerning his subjects, when affairs outside are disturbed he has only to fear that they will conspire secretly, from which a prince can easily secure himself by avoiding being hated and despised, and by keeping the people satisfied with him, which it is most necessary for him to accomplish, as I said above at length. And one of the most efficacious remedies that a prince can have against conspiracies is not to be hated and despised by the people, for he who conspires against a prince always expects to please them by his removal; but when the conspirator can only look forward to offending them, he will not have the courage to take such a course, for the difficulties that confront a conspirator are infinite. And as experience shows, many have been the conspiracies, but few have been successful; because he who conspires cannot act alone, nor can he take a companion except from those whom he believes to be malcontents, and as soon as you have opened your mind to a malcontent you have given him the material with which to content himself, for by denouncing you he can look for every advantage; so that, seeing the gain from this course to be assured, and seeing the other to be doubtful and full of dangers, he must be a very rare friend, or a thoroughly obstinate enemy of the prince, to keep faith with you.

And, to reduce the matter into a small compass, I say that, on the side of the conspirator, there is nothing but fear, jealousy, prospect of punishment to terrify him; but on the side of the prince there is the majesty of the principality, the laws, the protection of friends and the state to defend him; so that, adding to all these things the popular goodwill, it is impossible that any one should be so rash as to conspire. For whereas in general the conspirator has to fear before the execution of his plot, in this case he has also to fear the sequel to the crime; because on account of it he has the people for an enemy, and thus cannot hope for any escape.

Endless examples could be given on this subject, but I will be content with one, brought to pass within the memory of our fathers. Messer Annibale Bentivogli, who was prince in Bologna (grandfather of the present Annibale), having been murdered by the Canneschi, who had conspired against him, not one of his family survived but Messer Giovanni,[42] who was in childhood: immediately after his assassination the people rose and murdered all the Canneschi. This sprung from the popular goodwill which the house of Bentivogli enjoyed in those days in Bologna; which was so great that, although none remained there after the death of Annibale who was able to rule the state, the Bolognese, having information that there was one of the Bentivogli family in Florence, who up to that time had been considered the son of a blacksmith, sent to Florence for him and gave him the government of their city, and it was ruled by him until Messer Giovanni came in due course to the government.

For this reason I consider that a prince ought to reckon conspiracies of little account when his people hold him in esteem; but when it is hostile to him, and bears hatred towards him, he ought to fear everything and everybody. And well-ordered states and wise princes have taken every care not to drive the nobles to desperation, and to keep the people satisfied and contented, for this is one of the most important objects a prince can have.

---

[42] Giovanni Bentivogli, born in Bologna 1438, died at Milan 1508. He ruled Bologna from 1462 to 1506. Machiavelli's strong condemnation of conspiracies may get its edge from his own very recent experience (February 1513), when he had been arrested and tortured for his alleged complicity in the Boscoli conspiracy.

Among the best ordered and governed kingdoms of our times is France, and in it are found many good institutions on which depend the liberty and security of the king; of these the first is the parliament and its authority, because he who founded the kingdom, knowing the ambition of the nobility and their boldness, considered that a bit to their mouths would be necessary to hold them in; and, on the other side, knowing the hatred of the people, founded in fear, against the nobles, he wished to protect them, yet he was not anxious for this to be the particular care of the king; therefore, to take away the reproach which he would be liable to from the nobles for favouring the people, and from the people for favouring the nobles, he set up an arbiter, who should be one who could beat down the great and favour the lesser without reproach to the king. Neither could you have a better or a more prudent arrangement, or a greater source of security to the king and kingdom. From this one can draw another important conclusion, that princes ought to leave affairs of reproach to the management of others, and keep those of grace in their own hands. And further, I consider that a prince ought to cherish the nobles, but not so as to make himself hated by the people.

It may appear, perhaps, to some who have examined the lives and deaths of the Roman emperors that many of them would be an example contrary to my opinion, seeing that some of them lived nobly and showed great qualities of soul, nevertheless they have lost their empire or have been killed by subjects who have conspired against them. Wishing, therefore, to answer these objections, I will recall the characters of some of the emperors, and will show that the causes of their ruin were not different to those alleged by me; at the same time I will only submit for consideration those things that are noteworthy to him who studies the affairs of those times.

It seems to me sufficient to take all those emperors who succeeded to the empire from Marcus the philosopher down to Maximinus; they were Marcus and his son Commodus, Pertinax, Julian, Severus and his son Antoninus Caracalla, Macrinus, Heliogabalus, Alexander, and Maximinus.

There is first to note that, whereas in other principalities the ambition of the nobles and the insolence of the people only have to be contended with, the Roman emperors had a third difficulty in having to put up with the cruelty and avarice of their soldiers, a matter so beset with difficulties that it was the ruin of many; for it was a hard thing to give satisfaction both to soldiers and people; because the people loved peace, and for this reason they loved the unaspiring prince, whilst the soldiers loved the warlike prince who was bold, cruel, and rapacious, which qualities they were quite willing he should exercise upon the people, so that they could get double pay and give vent to their own greed and cruelty. Hence it arose that those emperors were always overthrown who, either by birth or training, had no great authority, and most of them, especially those who came new to the principality, recognizing the difficulty of these two opposing humours, were inclined to give satisfaction to the soldiers, caring little about injuring the people. Which course was necessary, because, as princes cannot help being hated by someone, they ought, in the first place, to avoid being hated by every one, and when they cannot compass this, they ought to endeavour with the utmost diligence to avoid the hatred of the most powerful. Therefore, those emperors who through inexperience had need of special favour adhered more readily to the soldiers than to the people; a course which turned out advantageous to them or not, accordingly as the prince knew how to maintain authority over them.

From these causes it arose that Marcus, Pertinax, and Alexander, being all men of modest life, lovers of justice, enemies to cruelty, humane, and benignant, came to a sad end except Marcus; he alone lived and died honoured, because he had succeeded to the throne by hereditary title, and owed nothing either to the soldiers or the people; and afterwards, being possessed of many virtues which made him respected, he always kept both orders in their places whilst he lived, and was neither hated nor despised.

But Pertinax was created emperor against the wishes of the soldiers, who, being accustomed to live licentiously under Commodus, could not endure the honest life to which Pertinax wished to reduce them; thus, having given cause for hatred, to which hatred there was added contempt for his old age, he was overthrown at the very beginning of his administration. And here it should be noted that hatred is acquired as much by good works as by bad ones, therefore, as I said before, a prince wishing to keep his state is very often forced to do evil; for when that body is corrupt whom you think you have need of to maintain yourself—it may be either the people or the soldiers or the nobles—you have to submit to its humours and to gratify them, and then good works will do you harm.

But let us come to Alexander, who was a man of such great goodness, that among the other praises which are accorded him is this, that in the fourteen years he held the empire no one was ever put to death by him unjudged; nevertheless, being considered effeminate and a man who allowed himself to be governed by his mother, he became despised, the army conspired against him, and murdered him.

Turning now to the opposite characters of Commodus, Severus, Antoninus Caracalla, and Maximinus, you will find them all cruel and rapacious-men who, to satisfy their soldiers, did not hesitate to commit every kind of iniquity against the people; and all, except Severus, came to a bad end; but in Severus there was so much valour that, keeping the soldiers friendly, although the people were oppressed by him, he reigned successfully; for his valour made him so much admired in the sight of the soldiers and people that the latter were kept in a way astonished and awed and the former respectful and satisfied. And because the actions of this man, as a new prince, were great, I wish to show briefly that he knew well how to counterfeit the fox and the lion, which natures, as I said above, it is necessary for a prince to imitate.

Knowing the sloth of the Emperor Julian, he persuaded the army in Sclavonia, of which he was captain, that it would be right to go to Rome and avenge the death of Pertinax, who had been killed by the praetorian soldiers; and under this pretext, without appearing to aspire to the throne, he moved the army on Rome, and reached Italy before it was known that he had started. On his arrival at Rome, the Senate, through fear, elected him emperor and killed Julian. After this there remained for Severus, who wished to make himself master of the whole empire, two difficulties; one in Asia, where Niger, head of the Asiatic army, had caused himself to be proclaimed emperor; the other in the west where Albinus was, who also aspired to the throne. And as he considered it dangerous to declare himself hostile to both, he decided to attack Niger and to deceive Albinus. To the latter he wrote that, being elected emperor by the Senate, he was willing to share that dignity with him and sent him the title of Caesar; and, moreover, that the Senate had made Albinus his colleague; which things were accepted by Albinus as true. But after Severus had conquered and killed Niger, and settled oriental affairs, he returned to Rome and complained to the Senate that Albinus, little recognizing the benefits that he had received from him, had by treachery sought to murder him, and for this ingratitude he was compelled to punish him. Afterwards he sought him out in France, and took from him his government and life. He who will, therefore, carefully examine the actions of this man will find him a most valiant lion and a most cunning fox; he will find him feared and respected by every one, and not hated by the army; and it need not be wondered at that he, a new man, was able to hold the empire so well, because his supreme renown always protected him from that hatred which the people might have conceived against him for his violence.

But his son Antoninus was a most eminent man, and had very excellent qualities, which made him admirable in the sight of the people and acceptable to the soldiers, for he was a warlike man, most enduring of fatigue, a despiser of all delicate food and other luxuries, which caused him to be beloved by the armies. Nevertheless, his ferocity and cruelties were so great and so unheard of that, after endless single murders, he killed a large number of the people of Rome and all those of Alexandria. He became hated by the whole world, and also feared by those he had around him, to such an extent that he was murdered in the midst of his army by a centurion. And here it must be noted that such-like deaths, which are deliberately inflicted with a resolved and desperate courage, cannot be avoided by princes, because any one who does not fear to die can inflict them; but a prince may fear them the less because they are very rare; he has only to be careful not to do any grave injury to those whom he employs or has around him in the service of the state. Antoninus had not taken this care, but had contumeliously killed a brother of that centurion, whom also he daily threatened, yet retained in his bodyguard; which, as it turned out, was a rash thing to do, and proved the emperor's ruin.

But let us come to Commodus, to whom it should have been very easy to hold the empire, for, being the son of Marcus, he had inherited it, and he had only to follow in the footsteps of his father to please his people and soldiers; but, being by nature cruel and brutal, he gave himself up to amusing the soldiers and corrupting them, so that he might indulge his rapacity upon the people; on the other hand, not maintaining his dignity, often descending to the theatre to compete with gladiators, and doing other vile things, little worthy of the imperial majesty, he fell into contempt with the soldiers, and being hated by one party and despised by the other, he was conspired against and was killed.

It remains to discuss the character of Maximinus. He was a very warlike man, and the armies, being disgusted with the effeminacy of Alexander, of whom I have already spoken, killed him and elected Maximinus to the throne. This he did not possess for long, for two things made him hated and despised; the one, his having kept sheep in Thrace, which brought him into contempt (it being well known to all, and considered a great indignity by every one), and the other, his having at the accession to his dominions deferred going to Rome and taking possession of the imperial seat; he had also gained a reputation for the utmost ferocity by having, through his prefects in Rome and elsewhere in the empire, practised many cruelties, so that the whole world was moved to anger at the meanness of his birth and to fear at his barbarity. First Africa rebelled, then the Senate with all the people of Rome, and all Italy conspired against him, to which may be added his own army; this latter, besieging Aquileia and meeting with difficulties in taking it, were disgusted with his cruelties, and fearing him less when they found so many against him, murdered him.

I do not wish to discuss Heliogabalus, Macrinus, or Julian, who, being thoroughly contemptible, were quickly wiped out; but I will bring this discourse to a conclusion by saying that princes in our times have this difficulty of giving inordinate satisfaction to their soldiers in a far less degree, because, notwithstanding one has to give them some indulgence, that is soon done; none of these princes have armies that are veterans in the governance and administration of provinces, as were the armies of the Roman Empire; and whereas it was then more necessary to give satisfaction to the soldiers than to the people, it is now more necessary to all princes, except the Turk and the Soldan, to satisfy the people rather the soldiers, because the people are the more powerful.

From the above I have excepted the Turk, who always keeps round him twelve thousand infantry and fifteen thousand cavalry on which depend the security and strength of the kingdom, and it is necessary that, putting aside every consideration for the people, he should keep them his friends. The kingdom of the Soldan is similar; being entirely in the hands of soldiers, it follows again that, without regard to the people, he must keep them his friends. But you must note that the state of the Soldan is unlike all other principalities, for the reason that it is like the Christian pontificate, which cannot be called either an hereditary or a newly formed principality; because the sons of the old prince are not the heirs, but he who is elected to that position by those who have authority, and the sons remain only noblemen. And this being an ancient custom, it cannot be called a new principality, because there are none of those difficulties in it that are met with in new ones; for although the prince is new, the constitution of the state is old, and it is framed so as to receive him as if he were its hereditary lord.

But returning to the subject of our discourse, I say that whoever will consider it will acknowledge that either hatred or contempt has been fatal to the above-named emperors, and it will be recognized also how it happened that, a number of them acting in one way and a number in another, only one in each way came to a happy end and the rest to unhappy ones. Because it would have been useless and dangerous for Pertinax and Alexander, being new princes, to imitate Marcus, who was heir to the principality; and likewise it would have been utterly destructive to Caracalla, Commodus, and Maximinus to have imitated Severus, they not having sufficient valour to enable them to tread in his footsteps. Therefore a prince, new to the principality, cannot imitate the actions of Marcus, nor, again, is it necessary to follow those of Severus, but he ought to take from Severus those parts which are necessary to found his state, and from Marcus those which are proper and glorious to keep a state that may already be stable and firm.

Chapter XX
ARE FORTRESSES, AND MANY OTHER THINGS TO WHICH PRINCES OFTEN RESORT, ADVANTAGEOUS OR HURTFUL?

1. Some princes, so as to hold securely the state, have disarmed their subjects; others have kept their subject towns distracted by factions; others have fostered enmities against themselves; others have laid themselves out to gain over those whom they distrusted in the beginning of their governments; some have built fortresses; some have overthrown and destroyed them. And although one cannot give a final judgment on all of these things unless one possesses the particulars of those states in which a decision has to be made, nevertheless I will speak as comprehensively as the matter of itself will admit.
2. There never was a new prince who has disarmed his subjects; rather when he has found them disarmed he has always armed them, because, by arming them, those arms become yours, those men who were distrusted become faithful, and those who were faithful are kept so, and your subjects become your adherents. And whereas all subjects cannot be armed, yet when those whom you do arm are benefited, the others can be handled more freely, and this difference in their treatment, which they quite understand, makes the former your dependents, and the latter, considering it to be necessary that those who have the most danger and service should have the most reward, excuse

you. But when you disarm them, you at once offend them by showing that you distrust them, either for cowardice or for want of loyalty, and either of these opinions breeds hatred against you. And because you cannot remain unarmed, it follows that you turn to mercenaries, which are of the character already shown; even if they should be good they would not be sufficient to defend you against powerful enemies and distrusted subjects. Therefore, as I have said, a new prince in a new principality has always distributed arms. Histories are full of examples. But when a prince acquires a new state, which he adds as a province to his old one, then it is necessary to disarm the men of that state, except those who have been his adherents in acquiring it; and these again, with time and opportunity, should be rendered soft and effeminate; and matters should be managed in such a way that all the armed men in the state shall be your own soldiers who in your old state were living near you.

3. Our forefathers, and those who were reckoned wise, were accustomed to say that it was necessary to hold Pistoia by factions and Pisa by fortresses; and with this idea they fostered quarrels in some of their tributary towns so as to keep possession of them the more easily. This may have been well enough in those times when Italy was in a way balanced, but I do not believe that it can be accepted as a precept for to-day, because I do not believe that factions can ever be of use; rather it is certain that when the enemy comes upon you in divided cities you are quickly lost, because the weakest party will always assist the outside forces and the other will not be able to resist. The Venetians, moved, as I believe, by the above reasons, fostered the Guelph and Ghibelline factions in their tributary cities; and although they never allowed them to come to bloodshed, yet they nursed these disputes amongst them, so that the citizens, distracted by their differences, should not unite against them. Which, as we saw, did not afterwards turn out as expected, because, after the rout at Vaila, one party at once took courage and seized the state. Such methods argue, therefore, weakness in the prince, because these factions will never be permitted in a vigorous principality; such methods for enabling one the more easily to manage subjects are only useful in times of peace, but if war comes this policy proves fallacious.

4. Without doubt princes become great when they overcome the difficulties and obstacles by which they are confronted, and therefore fortune, especially when she desires to make a new prince great, who has a greater necessity to earn renown than an hereditary one, causes enemies to arise and form designs against him, in order that he may have the opportunity of overcoming them, and by them to mount higher, as by a ladder which his enemies have raised. For this reason many consider that a wise prince, when he has the opportunity, ought with craft to foster some animosity against himself, so that, having crushed it, his renown may rise higher.

5. Princes, especially new ones, have found more fidelity and assistance in those men who in the beginning of their rule were distrusted than among those who in the beginning were trusted. Pandolfo Petrucci, Prince of Siena, ruled his state more by those who had been distrusted than by others. But on this question one cannot speak generally, for it varies so much with the individual; I will only say this, that those men who at the commencement of a princedom have been hostile, if they are of a description to need assistance to support themselves, can always be gained over with the greatest ease, and they will be tightly held to serve the prince with fidelity, inasmuch as they know it to be very necessary for them to cancel by deeds the bad impression which he had formed of them; and thus the prince always extracts more profit from them than from those who, serving him in too much security, may neglect his affairs. And since the matter demands it, I must not fail to warn a prince, who by means of secret favours has acquired a new state, that he must well consider the reasons which induced those to favour him who did so; and if it be not a natural affection towards him, but only discontent with their government, then he will only keep them friendly with great trouble and difficulty, for it will be impossible to satisfy them. And weighing well the reasons for this in those examples which can be taken from ancient and modern affairs, we shall find that it is easier for the prince to make friends of those men who were contented under the former government, and are therefore his enemies, than of those who, being discontented with it, were favourable to him and encouraged him to seize it.

6. It has been a custom with princes, in order to hold their states more securely, to build fortresses that may serve as a bridle and bit to those who might design to work against them, and as a place of refuge from a first attack. I praise this system because it has been made use of formerly. Notwithstanding that, Messer Nicolo Vitelli in our times has been seen to demolish two fortresses in Citta di Castello so that he might keep that state; Guido Ubaldo, Duke of Urbino, on returning to his dominion, whence he had been driven by Cesare Borgia, razed to the foundations all the fortresses in that province, and considered that without them it would be more difficult to lose it; the Bentivogli returning to Bologna came to a similar decision. Fortresses, therefore, are useful or not according to circumstances; if they do you good in one way they injure you in another. And this question can be reasoned thus: the prince who has more to fear from the people than from foreigners ought to build fortresses, but he who has more to fear from foreigners than from the people ought to leave them alone. The castle of Milan, built by Francesco Sforza, has made, and will make, more trouble for the house of Sforza than any other disorder in the state. For this reason the best possible fortress is—not to be hated by the people, because, although you may hold the fortresses, yet they will not save you if the people hate you, for there will never be wanting foreigners to assist a people who have taken arms against you. It has not been seen in our times that such fortresses have been of use to any prince, unless to the Countess of Forli,[43] when the Count Girolamo, her consort, was killed; for by that means she was able to withstand the popular attack and wait for assistance from Milan, and thus recover her state; and the posture of affairs was such at that time that the foreigners could not assist the people. But fortresses were of little value to her afterwards when Cesare Borgia attacked her, and when the people, her enemy, were allied with foreigners. Therefore, it would have been safer for her, both then and before, not to have been hated by the people than to have had the fortresses. All these things considered then, I shall praise him who builds fortresses as well as him who does not, and I shall blame whoever, trusting in them, cares little about being hated by the people.

[43] Catherine Sforza, a daughter of Galeazzo Sforza and Lucrezia Landriani, born 1463, died 1509. It was to the Countess of Forli that Machiavelli was sent as envoy on 1499. A letter from Fortunati to the countess announces the appointment: "I have been with the signori," wrote Fortunati, "to learn whom they would send and when. They tell me that Nicolo Machiavelli, a learned young Florentine noble, secretary to my Lords of the Ten, is to leave with me at once." *Cf.* "Catherine Sforza," by Count Pasolini, translated by P. Sylvester, 1898.

Chapter XXI
HOW A PRINCE SHOULD CONDUCT HIMSELF SO AS TO GAIN RENOWN

Nothing makes a prince so much esteemed as great enterprises and setting a fine example. We have in our time Ferdinand of Aragon, the present King of Spain. He can almost be called a new prince, because he has risen, by fame and glory, from being an insignificant king to be the foremost king in Christendom; and if you will consider his deeds you will find them all great and some of them extraordinary. In the beginning of his reign he attacked Granada, and this enterprise was the foundation of his dominions. He did this quietly at first and without any fear of hindrance, for he held the minds of the barons of Castile occupied in thinking of the war and not anticipating any innovations; thus they did not perceive that by these means he was acquiring power and authority over them. He was able with the money of the Church and of the people to sustain his armies, and by that long war to lay the foundation for the military skill which has since distinguished him. Further, always using religion as a plea, so as to undertake greater schemes, he devoted himself with pious cruelty to driving out and clearing his kingdom of the Moors; nor could there be a more admirable example, nor one more rare. Under this same cloak he assailed Africa, he came down on Italy, he has finally attacked France; and thus his achievements and designs have always been great, and have kept the minds of his people in suspense and admiration and occupied with the issue of them. And his actions have arisen in such a way, one out of the other, that men have never been given time to work steadily against him.

Again, it much assists a prince to set unusual examples in internal affairs, similar to those which are related of Messer Bernabo da Milano, who, when he had the opportunity, by any one in civil life doing some extraordinary thing, either good or bad, would take some method of rewarding or punishing him, which would be much spoken about. And a prince ought, above all things, always endeavour in every action to gain for himself the reputation of being a great and remarkable man.

A prince is also respected when he is either a true friend or a downright enemy, that is to say, when, without any reservation, he declares himself in favour of one party against the other; which course will always be more advantageous than standing neutral; because if two of your powerful neighbours come to blows, they are of such a character that, if one of them conquers, you have either to fear him or not. In either case it will always be more advantageous for you to declare yourself and to make war strenuously; because, in the first case, if you do not declare yourself, you will invariably fall a prey to the conqueror, to the pleasure and satisfaction of him who has been conquered, and you will have no reasons to offer, nor anything to protect or to shelter you. Because he who conquers does not want doubtful friends who will not aid him in the time of trial; and he who loses will not harbour you because you did not willingly, sword in hand, court his fate.

Antiochus went into Greece, being sent for by the Ætolians to drive out the Romans. He sent envoys to the Achaeans, who were friends of the Romans, exhorting them to remain neutral; and on the other hand the Romans urged them to take up arms. This question came to be discussed in the council of the Achaeans, where the legate of Antiochus urged them to stand neutral. To this the Roman legate answered: "As for that which has been said, that it is better and more advantageous for your state not to interfere in our war, nothing can be more erroneous; because by not interfering you will be left, without favour or consideration, the guerdon of the conqueror." Thus it will always happen that he who is not your friend will demand your neutrality, whilst he who is your friend will entreat you to declare yourself with arms. And irresolute princes, to avoid present dangers, generally follow the neutral path, and are generally ruined. But when a prince declares himself gallantly in favour of one side, if the party with whom he allies himself conquers, although the victor may be powerful and may have him at his mercy, yet he is indebted to him, and there is established a bond of amity; and men are never so shameless as to become a monument of ingratitude by oppressing you. Victories after all are never so complete that the victor must not show some regard, especially to justice. But if he with whom you ally yourself loses, you may be sheltered by him, and whilst he is able he may aid you, and you become companions on a fortune that may rise again.

In the second case, when those who fight are of such a character that you have no anxiety as to who may conquer, so much the more is it greater prudence to be allied, because you assist at the destruction of one by the aid of another who, if he had been wise, would have saved him; and conquering, as it is impossible that he should not do with your assistance, he remains at your discretion. And here it is to be noted that a prince ought to take care never to make an alliance with one more powerful than himself for the purposes of attacking others, unless necessity compels him, as is said above; because if he conquers you are at his discretion, and princes ought to avoid as much as possible being at the discretion of any one. The Venetians joined with France against the Duke of Milan, and this alliance, which caused their ruin, could have been avoided. But when it cannot be avoided, as happened to the Florentines when the Pope and Spain sent armies to attack Lombardy, then in such a case, for the above reasons, the prince ought to favour one of the parties.

Never let any Government imagine that it can choose perfectly safe courses; rather let it expect to have to take very doubtful ones, because it is found in ordinary affairs that one never seeks to avoid one trouble without running into another; but prudence consists in knowing how to distinguish the character of troubles, and for choice to take the lesser evil.

A prince ought also to show himself a patron of ability, and to honour the proficient in every art. At the same time he should encourage his citizens to practise their callings peaceably, both in commerce and agriculture, and in every other following, so that the one should not be deterred from improving his possessions for fear lest they be taken away from him or another from opening up trade for fear of taxes; but the prince ought to offer rewards to whoever wishes to do these things and designs in any way to honour his city or state.

Further, he ought to entertain the people with festivals and spectacles at convenient seasons of the year; and as every city is divided into guilds or into societies,[44] he ought to hold such bodies in esteem, and associate with them sometimes, and show himself an example of courtesy and liberality; nevertheless, always maintaining the majesty of his rank, for this he must never consent to abate in anything.

---

[44] "Guilds or societies," "in arti o in tribu." "Arti" were craft or trade guilds, *cf.* Florio: "Arte... a whole company of any trade in any city or corporation town." The guilds of Florence are most admirably described by Mr Edgcumbe Staley in his work on the subject (Methuen, 1906). Institutions of a somewhat similar character, called "artel," exist in Russia to-day, *cf.* Sir Mackenzie Wallace's "Russia," ed. 1905: "The sons... were always during the working season members of an artel. In some of the larger towns there are artels of a much more complex kind— permanent associations, possessing large capital, and pecuniarily responsible for the acts of the individual members." The word "artel," despite its apparent similarity, has, Mr Aylmer Maude assures me, no connection with "ars" or "arte." Its root is that of the verb "rotisya," to bind oneself by an oath; and it is generally admitted to be only another form of "rota," which now signifies a "regimental company." In both words the underlying idea is that of a body of men united by an oath. "Tribu" were possibly gentile groups, united by common descent, and included individuals connected by marriage. Perhaps our words "sects" or "clans" would be most appropriate.

Chapter XXII
CONCERNING THE SECRETARIES OF PRINCES

The choice of servants is of no little importance to a prince, and they are good or not according to the discrimination of the prince. And the first opinion which one forms of a prince, and of his understanding, is by observing the men he has around him; and when they are capable and faithful he may always be considered wise, because he has known how to recognize the capable and to keep them faithful. But when they are otherwise one cannot form a good opinion of him, for the prime error which he made was in choosing them.

There were none who knew Messer Antonio da Venafro as the servant of Pandolfo Petrucci, Prince of Siena, who would not consider Pandolfo to be a very clever man in having Venafro for his servant. Because there are three classes of intellects: one which comprehends by itself; another which appreciates what others comprehended; and a third which neither comprehends by itself nor by the showing of others; the first is the most excellent, the second is good, the third is useless. Therefore, it follows necessarily that, if Pandolfo was not in the first rank, he was in the second, for whenever one has judgment to know good and bad when it is said and done, although he himself may not have the initiative, yet he can recognize the good and the bad in his servant, and the one he can praise and the other correct; thus the servant cannot hope to deceive him, and is kept honest.

But to enable a prince to form an opinion of his servant there is one test which never fails; when you see the servant thinking more of his own interests than of yours, and seeking inwardly his own profit in everything, such a man will never make a good servant, nor will you ever be able to trust him; because he who has the state of another in his hands ought never to think of himself, but always of his prince, and never pay any attention to matters in which the prince is not concerned.

On the other hand, to keep his servant honest the prince ought to study him, honouring him, enriching him, doing him kindnesses, sharing with him the honours and cares; and at the same time let him see that he cannot stand alone, so that many honours may not make him desire more, many riches make him wish for more, and that many cares may make him dread chances. When, therefore, servants, and princes towards servants, are thus disposed, they can trust each other, but when it is otherwise, the end will always be disastrous for either one or the other.

Chapter XXIII
HOW FLATTERERS SHOULD BE AVOIDED

I do not wish to leave out an important branch of this subject, for it is a danger from which princes are with difficulty preserved, unless they are very careful and discriminating. It is that of flatterers, of whom courts are full, because men are so self-complacent in their own affairs, and in a way so deceived in them, that they are preserved with difficulty from this pest, and if they wish to defend themselves they run the danger of falling into contempt. Because there is no other way of guarding oneself from flatterers except letting men understand that to tell you the truth does not offend you; but when every one may tell you the truth, respect for you abates.

Therefore a wise prince ought to hold a third course by choosing the wise men in his state, and giving to them only the liberty of speaking the truth to him, and then only of those things of which he inquires, and of none others; but he ought to question them upon everything, and listen to their opinions, and afterwards form his own conclusions. With these councillors, separately and collectively, he ought to carry himself in such a way that each of them should know that, the more freely he shall speak, the more he shall be preferred; outside of these, he should listen to no one, pursue the thing resolved on, and be steadfast in his resolutions. He who does otherwise is either overthrown by flatterers, or is so often changed by varying opinions that he falls into contempt.

I wish on this subject to adduce a modern example. Fra Luca, the man of affairs to Maximilian,[45] the present emperor, speaking of his majesty, said: He consulted with no one, yet never got his own way in anything. This arose because of his following a practice the opposite to the above; for the emperor is a secretive man—he does not communicate his designs to any one, nor does he receive opinions on them. But as in carrying them into effect they become revealed and known, they are at once obstructed by those men whom he has around him, and he, being pliant, is diverted from them. Hence it follows that those things he does one day he undoes the next, and no one ever understands what he wishes or intends to do, and no one can rely on his resolutions.

A prince, therefore, ought always to take counsel, but only when he wishes and not when others wish; he ought rather to discourage every one from offering advice unless he asks it; but, however, he ought to be a constant inquirer, and afterwards a patient listener concerning the things of which he inquired; also, on learning that any one, on any consideration, has not told him the truth, he should let his anger be felt.

And if there are some who think that a prince who conveys an impression of his wisdom is not so through his own ability, but through the good advisers that he has around him, beyond doubt they are deceived, because this is an axiom which never fails: that a prince who is not wise himself will never take good advice, unless by chance he has yielded his affairs entirely to one person who happens to be a very prudent man. In this case indeed he may be well governed, but it would not be for long, because such a governor would in a short time take away his state from him.

But if a prince who is not inexperienced should take counsel from more than one he will never get united counsels, nor will he know how to unite them. Each of the counsellors will think of his

[45] Maximilian I, born in 1459, died 1519, Emperor of the Holy Roman Empire. He married, first, Mary, daughter of Charles the Bold; after her death, Bianca Sforza; and thus became involved in Italian politics.

own interests, and the prince will not know how to control them or to see through them. And they are not to be found otherwise, because men will always prove untrue to you unless they are kept honest by constraint. Therefore it must be inferred that good counsels, whencesoever they come, are born of the wisdom of the prince, and not the wisdom of the prince from good counsels.

Chapter XXIV
WHY THE PRINCES OF ITALY HAVE LOST THEIR STATES

The previous suggestions, carefully observed, will enable a new prince to appear well established, and render him at once more secure and fixed in the state than if he had been long seated there. For the actions of a new prince are more narrowly observed than those of an hereditary one, and when they are seen to be able they gain more men and bind far tighter than ancient blood; because men are attracted more by the present than by the past, and when they find the present good they enjoy it and seek no further; they will also make the utmost defence of a prince if he fails them not in other things. Thus it will be a double glory for him to have established a new principality, and adorned and strengthened it with good laws, good arms, good allies, and with a good example; so will it be a double disgrace to him who, born a prince, shall lose his state by want of wisdom.

And if those seigniors are considered who have lost their states in Italy in our times, such as the King of Naples, the Duke of Milan, and others, there will be found in them, firstly, one common defect in regard to arms from the causes which have been discussed at length; in the next place, some one of them will be seen, either to have had the people hostile, or if he has had the people friendly, he has not known how to secure the nobles. In the absence of these defects states that have power enough to keep an army in the field cannot be lost.

Philip of Macedon, not the father of Alexander the Great, but he who was conquered by Titus Quintius, had not much territory compared to the greatness of the Romans and of Greece who attacked him, yet being a warlike man who knew how to attract the people and secure the nobles, he sustained the war against his enemies for many years, and if in the end he lost the dominion of some cities, nevertheless he retained the kingdom.

Therefore, do not let our princes accuse fortune for the loss of their principalities after so many years' possession, but rather their own sloth, because in quiet times they never thought there could be a change (it is a common defect in man not to make any provision in the calm against the tempest), and when afterwards the bad times came they thought of flight and not of defending themselves, and they hoped that the people, disgusted with the insolence of the conquerors, would recall them. This course, when others fail, may be good, but it is very bad to have neglected all other expedients for that, since you would never wish to fall because you trusted to be able to find someone later on to restore you. This again either does not happen, or, if it does, it will not be for your security, because that deliverance is of no avail which does not depend upon yourself; those only are reliable, certain, and durable that depend on yourself and your valour.

Chapter XXV
WHAT FORTUNE CAN EFFECT IN HUMAN AFFAIRS AND HOW TO WITHSTAND HER

It is not unknown to me how many men have had, and still have, the opinion that the affairs of the world are in such wise governed by fortune and by God that men with their wisdom cannot direct them and that no one can even help them; and because of this they would have us believe that it is not necessary to labour much in affairs, but to let chance govern them. This opinion has been more credited in our times because of the great changes in affairs which have been seen, and may still be seen, every day, beyond all human conjecture. Sometimes pondering over this, I am in some degree inclined to their opinion. Nevertheless, not to extinguish our free will, I hold it to be true that Fortune is the arbiter of one-half of our actions,[46] but that she still leaves us to direct the other half, or perhaps a little less.

I compare her to one of those raging rivers, which when in flood overflows the plains, sweeping away trees and buildings, bearing away the soil from place to place; everything flies before it, all yield to its violence, without being able in any way to withstand it; and yet, though its nature be such, it does not follow therefore that men,

[46] Frederick the Great was accustomed to say: "The older one gets the more convinced one becomes that his Majesty King Chance does three-quarters of the business of this miserable universe." Sorel's "Eastern Question."

when the weather becomes fair, shall not make provision, both with defences and barriers, in such a manner that, rising again, the waters may pass away by canal, and their force be neither so unrestrained nor so dangerous. So it happens with fortune, who shows her power where valour has not prepared to resist her, and thither she turns her forces where she knows that barriers and defences have not been raised to constrain her.

And if you will consider Italy, which is the seat of these changes, and which has given to them their impulse, you will see it to be an open country without barriers and without any defence. For if it had been defended by proper valour, as are Germany, Spain, and France, either this invasion would not have made the great changes it has made or it would not have come at all. And this I consider enough to say concerning resistance to fortune in general.

But confining myself more to the particular, I say that a prince may be seen happy to-day and ruined to-morrow without having shown any change of disposition or character. This, I believe, arises firstly from causes that have already been discussed at length, namely, that the prince who relies entirely on fortune is lost when it changes. I believe also that he will be successful who directs his actions according to the spirit of the times, and that he whose actions do not accord with the times will not be successful. Because men are seen, in affairs that lead to the end which every man has before him, namely, glory and riches, to get there by various methods; one with caution, another with haste; one by force, another by skill; one by patience, another by its opposite; and each one succeeds in reaching the goal by a different method. One can also see of two cautious men the one attain his end, the other fail; and similarly, two men by different observances are equally successful, the one being cautious, the other impetuous; all this arises from nothing else than whether or not they conform in their methods to the spirit of the times. This follows from what I have said, that two men working differently bring about the same effect, and of two working similarly, one attains his object and the other does not.

Changes in estate also issue from this, for if, to one who governs himself with caution and patience, times and affairs converge in such a way that his administration is successful, his fortune is made; but if times and affairs change, he is ruined if he does not change his course of action. But a man is not often found sufficiently circumspect to know how to accommodate himself to the change, both because he cannot deviate from what nature inclines him to do, and also because, having always prospered by acting in one way, he cannot be persuaded that it is well to leave it; and, therefore, the cautious man, when it is time to turn adventurous, does not know how to do it, hence he is ruined; but had he changed his conduct with the times fortune would not have changed.

Pope Julius the Second went to work impetuously in all his affairs, and found the times and circumstances conform so well to that line of action that he always met with success. Consider his first enterprise against Bologna, Messer Giovanni Bentivogli being still alive. The Venetians were not agreeable to it, nor was the King of Spain, and he had the enterprise still under discussion with the King of France; nevertheless he personally entered upon the expedition with his accustomed boldness and energy, a move which made Spain and the Venetians stand irresolute and passive, the latter from fear, the former from desire to recover the kingdom of Naples; on the other hand, he drew after him the King of France, because that king, having observed the movement, and desiring to make the Pope his friend so as to humble the Venetians, found it impossible to refuse him. Therefore Julius with his impetuous action accomplished what no other pontiff with simple human wisdom could have done; for if he had waited in Rome until he could get away, with his plans arranged and everything fixed, as any other pontiff would have done, he would never have succeeded. Because the King of France would have made a thousand excuses, and the others would have raised a thousand fears.

I will leave his other actions alone, as they were all alike, and they all succeeded, for the shortness of his life did not let him experience the contrary; but if circumstances had arisen which required him to go cautiously, his ruin would have followed, because he would never have deviated from those ways to which nature inclined him.

I conclude, therefore that, fortune being changeful and mankind steadfast in their ways, so long as the two are in agreement men are successful, but unsuccessful when they fall out. For my part I consider that it is better to be adventurous than cautious, because fortune is a woman, and if you wish to keep her under it is necessary to beat and ill-use her; and it is seen that she allows herself to be mastered by the adventurous rather than by those who go to work more coldly. She is, therefore, always, woman-like, a lover of young men, because they are less cautious, more violent, and with more audacity command her.

Chapter XXVI
AN EXHORTATION TO LIBERATE ITALY FROM THE BARBARIANS

Having carefully considered the subject of the above discourses, and wondering within myself whether the present times were propitious to a new prince, and whether there were elements that would give an opportunity to a wise and virtuous one to introduce a new order of things which would do honour to him and good to the people of this country, it appears to me that so many things concur to favour a new prince that I never knew a time more fit than the present.

And if, as I said, it was necessary that the people of Israel should be captive so as to make manifest the ability of Moses; that the Persians should be oppressed by the Medes so as to discover the greatness of the soul of Cyrus; and that the Athenians should be dispersed to illustrate the capabilities of Theseus: then at the present time, in order to discover the virtue of an Italian spirit, it was necessary that Italy should be reduced to the extremity that she is now in, that she should be more enslaved than the Hebrews, more oppressed than the Persians, more scattered than the Athenians; without head, without order, beaten, despoiled, torn, overrun; and to have endured every kind of desolation.

Although lately some spark may have been shown by one, which made us think he was ordained by God for our redemption, nevertheless it was afterwards seen, in the height of his career, that fortune rejected him; so that Italy, left as without life, waits for him who shall yet heal her wounds and put an end to the ravaging and plundering of Lombardy, to the swindling and taxing of the kingdom and of Tuscany, and cleanse those sores that for long have festered. It is seen how she entreats God to send someone who shall deliver her from these wrongs and barbarous insolencies. It is seen also that she is ready and willing to follow a banner if only someone will raise it.

Nor is there to be seen at present one in whom she can place more hope than in your illustrious house,[47] with its valour and fortune, favoured by God and by the Church of which it is now the chief, and which could be made the head of this redemption. This will not be difficult if you will recall to yourself the actions and lives of the men I have named. And although they were great and wonderful men, yet they were men, and each one of them had no more opportunity than the present offers, for their enterprises were neither more just nor easier than this, nor was God more their friend than He is yours.

With us there is great justice, because that war is just which is necessary, and arms are hallowed when there is no other hope but in them. Here there is the greatest willingness, and where the willingness is great the difficulties cannot be great if you will only follow those men to whom I have directed your attention. Further than this, how extraordinarily the ways of God have been manifested beyond example: the sea is divided, a cloud has led the way, the rock has poured forth water, it has rained manna, everything has contributed to your greatness; you ought to do the rest. God is not willing to do everything, and thus take away our free will and that share of glory which belongs to us.

And it is not to be wondered at if none of the above-named Italians have been able to accomplish all that is expected from your

---

[47] Giuliano de Medici. He had just been created a cardinal by Leo X. In 1523 Giuliano was elected Pope, and took the title of Clement VII.

illustrious house; and if in so many revolutions in Italy, and in so many campaigns, it has always appeared as if military virtue were exhausted, this has happened because the old order of things was not good, and none of us have known how to find a new one. And nothing honours a man more than to establish new laws and new ordinances when he himself was newly risen. Such things when they are well founded and dignified will make him revered and admired, and in Italy there are not wanting opportunities to bring such into use in every form.

Here there is great valour in the limbs whilst it fails in the head. Look attentively at the duels and the hand-to-hand combats, how superior the Italians are in strength, dexterity, and subtlety. But when it comes to armies they do not bear comparison, and this springs entirely from the insufficiency of the leaders, since those who are capable are not obedient, and each one seems to himself to know, there having never been any one so distinguished above the rest, either by valour or fortune, that others would yield to him. Hence it is that for so long a time, and during so much fighting in the past twenty years, whenever there has been an army wholly Italian, it has always given a poor account of itself; the first witness to this is Il Taro, afterwards Allesandria, Capua, Genoa, Vaila, Bologna, Mestri.[48]

If, therefore, your illustrious house wishes to follow these remarkable men who have redeemed their country, it is necessary before all things, as a true foundation for every enterprise, to be provided with your own forces, because there can be no more faithful, truer, or better soldiers. And although singly they are good, altogether they will be much better when they find themselves commanded by their prince, honoured by him, and maintained at his expense. Therefore it is necessary to be prepared

[48] The battles of Il Taro, 1495; Alessandria, 1499; Capua, 1501; Genoa, 1507; Vaila, 1509; Bologna, 1511; Mestri, 1513.

with such arms, so that you can be defended against foreigners by Italian valour.

And although Swiss and Spanish infantry may be considered very formidable, nevertheless there is a defect in both, by reason of which a third order would not only be able to oppose them, but might be relied upon to overthrow them. For the Spaniards cannot resist cavalry, and the Switzers are afraid of infantry whenever they encounter them in close combat. Owing to this, as has been and may again be seen, the Spaniards are unable to resist French cavalry, and the Switzers are overthrown by Spanish infantry. And although a complete proof of this latter cannot be shown, nevertheless there was some evidence of it at the battle of Ravenna, when the Spanish infantry were confronted by German battalions, who follow the same tactics as the Swiss; when the Spaniards, by agility of body and with the aid of their shields, got in under the pikes of the Germans and stood out of danger, able to attack, while the Germans stood helpless, and, if the cavalry had not dashed up, all would have been over with them. It is possible, therefore, knowing the defects of both these infantries, to invent a new one, which will resist cavalry and not be afraid of infantry; this need not create a new order of arms, but a variation upon the old. And these are the kind of improvements which confer reputation and power upon a new prince.

This opportunity, therefore, ought not to be allowed to pass for letting Italy at last see her liberator appear. Nor can one express the love with which he would be received in all those provinces which have suffered so much from these foreign scourings, with what thirst for revenge, with what stubborn faith, with what devotion, with what tears. What door would be closed to him? Who would refuse obedience to him? What envy would hinder him? What Italian would refuse him homage? To all of us this barbarous dominion stinks. Let, therefore, your illustrious house take up this charge with that courage and hope with which all just enterprises are undertaken, so that under its standard our native country may be ennobled, and under its auspices may be verified that saying of Petrarch:

Virtu contro al Furore
Prendera l'arme, e fia il combatter corto:
Che l'antico valore
Negli italici cuor non e ancor morto.

Virtue against fury shall advance the fight,
And it i' th' combat soon shall put to flight:
For the old Roman valour is not dead,
Nor in th' Italians' brests extinguished.

Edward Dacre, 1640.

Description of the methods adopted by the Duke Valentino when murdering Vitellozzo Vitelli, Oliverotto Da Fermo, the Signor Pagolo, and the Duke Di Gravina Orsini

BY NICOLO MACHIAVELLI

The Duke Valentino had returned from Lombardy, where he had been to clear himself with the King of France from the calumnies which had been raised against him by the Florentines concerning the rebellion of Arezzo and other towns in the Val di Chiana, and had arrived at Imola, whence he intended with his army to enter upon the campaign against Giovanni Bentivogli, the tyrant of Bologna: for he intended to bring that city under his domination, and to make it the head of his Romagnian duchy.

These matters coming to the knowledge of the Vitelli and Orsini and their following, it appeared to them that the duke would become too powerful, and it was feared that, having seized Bologna, he would seek to destroy them in order that he might become supreme in Italy. Upon this a meeting was called at Magione in the district of Perugia, to which came the cardinal, Pagolo, and the Duke di Gravina Orsini, Vitellozzo Vitelli, Oliverotto da Fermo, Gianpagolo Baglioni, the tyrant of Perugia, and Messer Antonio da Venafro, sent by Pandolfo Petrucci, the Prince of Siena. Here were discussed the power and courage of the duke and the necessity of curbing his ambitions, which might otherwise bring danger to the rest of being ruined. And they decided not to abandon the Bentivogli, but to strive to win over the Florentines; and they sent their men to one place and another, promising to one party assistance and to another encouragement to unite with them against the common enemy. This meeting was at once reported throughout all Italy, and those who were discontented under the duke, among whom were the people of Urbino, took hope of effecting a revolution.

Thus it arose that, men's minds being thus unsettled, it was decided by certain men of Urbino to seize the fortress of San Leo, which was held for the duke, and which they captured by the following means. The castellan was fortifying the rock and causing timber to be taken there; so the conspirators watched, and when certain beams which were being carried to the rock were upon the bridge, so that it was prevented from being drawn up by those inside, they took the opportunity of leaping upon the bridge and thence into the fortress. Upon this capture being effected, the whole state rebelled and recalled the old duke, being encouraged in this, not so much by the capture of the fort, as by the Diet at Magione, from whom they expected to get assistance.

Those who heard of the rebellion at Urbino thought they would not lose the opportunity, and at once assembled their men so as to take any town, should any remain in the hands of the duke in that state; and they sent again to Florence to beg that republic to join with them in destroying the common firebrand, showing that the risk was lessened and that they ought not to wait for another opportunity.

But the Florentines, from hatred, for sundry reasons, of the Vitelli and Orsini, not only would not ally themselves, but sent Nicolo Machiavelli, their secretary, to offer shelter and assistance to the duke against his enemies. The duke was found full of fear at Imola, because, against everybody's expectation, his soldiers had at once gone over to the enemy and he found himself disarmed and war at his door. But recovering courage from the offers of the Florentines, he decided to temporize before fighting with the few soldiers that remained to him, and to negotiate for a reconciliation, and also to get assistance. This latter he obtained in two ways, by sending to the King of France for men and by enlisting men-at-arms and others whom he turned into cavalry of a sort: to all he gave money.

Notwithstanding this, his enemies drew near to him, and approached Fossombrone, where they encountered some men of the duke and, with the aid of the Orsini and Vitelli, routed them. When this happened, the duke resolved at once to see if he could not close the trouble with offers of reconciliation, and being a most perfect dissembler he did not fail in any practices to make the insurgents understand that he wished every man who had acquired anything to keep it, as it was enough for him to have the title of prince, whilst others might have the principality.

And the duke succeeded so well in this that they sent Signor Pagolo to him to negotiate for a reconciliation, and they brought their army to a standstill. But the duke did not stop his preparations, and took every care to provide himself with cavalry and infantry, and that such preparations might not be apparent to the others, he sent his troops in separate parties to every part of the Romagna. In the meanwhile there came also to him five hundred French lancers, and although he found himself sufficiently strong to take vengeance on his enemies in open war, he considered that it would be safer and more advantageous to outwit them, and for this reason he did not stop the work of reconciliation.

And that this might be effected the duke concluded a peace with them in which he confirmed their former covenants; he gave them four thousand ducats at once; he promised not to injure the Bentivogli; and he formed an alliance with Giovanni; and moreover he would not force them to come personally into his presence unless it pleased them to do so. On the other hand, they promised to restore to him the duchy of Urbino and other places seized by them, to serve him in all his expeditions, and not to make war against or ally themselves with any one without his permission.

This reconciliation being completed, Guido Ubaldo, the Duke of Urbino, again fled to Venice, having first destroyed all the fortresses in his state; because, trusting in the people, he did not wish that the fortresses, which he did not think he could defend, should be held by the enemy, since by these means a check would be kept upon his friends. But the Duke Valentino, having completed this convention, and dispersed his men throughout the Romagna, set out for Imola at the end of November together with his French men-at-arms: thence he went to Cesena, where he stayed some time to negotiate with the envoys of the Vitelli and Orsini, who had assembled with their men in the duchy of Urbino, as to the enterprise in which they should now take part; but nothing being concluded, Oliverotto da Fermo was sent to propose that if the duke wished to undertake an expedition against Tuscany they were ready; if he did not wish it, then they would besiege Sinigalia. To this the duke replied that he did not wish to enter into war with Tuscany, and thus become hostile to the Florentines, but that he was very willing to proceed against Sinigalia.

It happened that not long afterwards the town surrendered, but the fortress would not yield to them because the castellan would not give it up to any one but the duke in person; therefore they exhorted him to come there. This appeared a good opportunity to the duke, as, being invited by them, and not going of his own will, he would awaken no suspicions. And the more to reassure them, he allowed all the French men-at-arms who were with him in Lombardy to depart, except the hundred lancers under Mons. di Candales, his brother-in-law. He left Cesena about the middle of December, and went to Fano, and with the utmost cunning and cleverness he persuaded the Vitelli and Orsini to wait for him at Sinigalia, pointing out to them that any lack of compliance would cast a doubt upon the sincerity and permanency of the reconciliation, and that he was a man who wished to make use of the arms and councils of his friends. But Vitellozzo remained very stubborn, for the death of his brother warned him that he should not offend a prince and afterwards trust him; nevertheless, persuaded by Pagolo Orsini, whom the duke had corrupted with gifts and promises, he agreed to wait.

Upon this the duke, before his departure from Fano, which was to be on 30th December 1502, communicated his designs to eight of his most trusted followers, among whom were Don Michele and the Monsignor d'Euna, who was afterwards cardinal; and he ordered that, as soon as Vitellozzo, Pagolo Orsini, the Duke di Gravina, and Oliverotto should arrive, his followers in pairs should take them one by one, entrusting certain men to certain pairs, who should entertain them until they reached Sinigalia; nor should they be permitted to leave until they came to the duke's quarters, where they should be seized.

The duke afterwards ordered all his horsemen and infantry, of which there were more than two thousand cavalry and ten thousand footmen, to assemble by daybreak at the Metauro, a river five miles distant from Fano, and await him there. He found himself, therefore, on the last day of December at the Metauro with his men, and having sent a cavalcade of about two hundred horsemen before him, he then moved forward the infantry, whom he accompanied with the rest of the men-at-arms.

Fano and Sinigalia are two cities of La Marca situated on the shore of the Adriatic Sea, fifteen miles distant from each other, so that he who goes towards Sinigalia has the mountains on his right hand, the bases of which are touched by the sea in some places. The city of Sinigalia is distant from the foot of the mountains a little more than a bow-shot and from the shore about a mile. On the side opposite to the city runs a little river which bathes that part of the walls looking towards Fano, facing the high road. Thus he who draws near to Sinigalia comes for a good space by road along the mountains, and reaches the river which passes by Sinigalia. If he turns to his left hand along the bank of it, and goes for the distance of a bow-shot, he arrives at a bridge which crosses the river; he is then almost abreast of the gate that leads into Sinigalia, not by a straight line, but transversely. Before this gate there stands a collection of houses with a square to which the bank of the river forms one side.

The Vitelli and Orsini having received orders to wait for the duke, and to honour him in person, sent away their men to several castles distant from Sinigalia about six miles, so that room could be made for the men of the duke; and they left in Sinigalia only Oliverotto and his band, which consisted of one thousand infantry and one hundred and fifty horsemen, who were quartered in the suburb mentioned above. Matters having been thus arranged, the Duke Valentino left for Sinigalia, and when the leaders of the cavalry reached the bridge they did not pass over, but having opened it, one portion wheeled towards the river and the other towards the country, and a way was left in the middle through which the infantry passed, without stopping, into the town.

Vitellozzo, Pagolo, and the Duke di Gravina on mules, accompanied by a few horsemen, went towards the duke; Vitellozo, unarmed and wearing a cape lined with green, appeared very dejected, as if conscious of his approaching death—a circumstance which, in view of the ability of the man and his former fortune, caused some amazement. And it is said that when he parted from his men before setting out for Sinigalia to meet the duke he acted as if it were his last parting from them. He recommended his house and its fortunes to his captains, and advised his nephews that it was not the fortune of their house, but the virtues of their fathers that should be kept in mind. These three, therefore, came before the duke and saluted him respectfully, and were received by him with goodwill; they were at once placed between those who were commissioned to look after them.

But the duke noticing that Oliverotto, who had remained with his band in Sinigalia, was missing—for Oliverotto was waiting in the square before his quarters near the river, keeping his men in order and drilling them—signalled with his eye to Don Michelle, to whom the care of Oliverotto had been committed, that he should take measures that Oliverotto should not escape. Therefore Don

Michele rode off and joined Oliverotto, telling him that it was not right to keep his men out of their quarters, because these might be taken up by the men of the duke; and he advised him to send them at once to their quarters and to come himself to meet the duke. And Oliverotto, having taken this advice, came before the duke, who, when he saw him, called to him; and Oliverotto, having made his obeisance, joined the others.

So the whole party entered Sinigalia, dismounted at the duke's quarters, and went with him into a secret chamber, where the duke made them prisoners; he then mounted on horseback, and issued orders that the men of Oliverotto and the Orsini should be stripped of their arms. Those of Oliverotto, being at hand, were quickly settled, but those of the Orsini and Vitelli, being at a distance, and having a presentiment of the destruction of their masters, had time to prepare themselves, and bearing in mind the valour and discipline of the Orsinian and Vitellian houses, they stood together against the hostile forces of the country and saved themselves.

But the duke's soldiers, not being content with having pillaged the men of Oliverotto, began to sack Sinigalia, and if the duke had not repressed this outrage by killing some of them they would have completely sacked it. Night having come and the tumult being silenced, the duke prepared to kill Vitellozzo and Oliverotto; he led them into a room and caused them to be strangled. Neither of them used words in keeping with their past lives: Vitellozzo prayed that he might ask of the pope full pardon for his sins; Oliverotto cringed and laid the blame for all injuries against the duke on Vitellozzo. Pagolo and the Duke di Gravina Orsini were kept alive until the duke heard from Rome that the pope had taken the Cardinal Orsino, the Archbishop of Florence, and Messer Jacopo da Santa Croce. After which news, on 18th January 1502, in the castle of Pieve, they also were strangled in the same way.

The Life of Castruccio Castracani of Lucca

WRITTEN BY NICOLO MACHIAVELLI

And sent to his friends ZANOBI BUONDELMONTI and LUIGI ALAMANNI

CASTRUCCIO CASTRACANI 1284-1328

It appears, dearest Zanobi and Luigi, a wonderful thing to those who have considered the matter, that all men, or the larger number of them, who have performed great deeds in the world, and excelled all others in their day, have had their birth and beginning in baseness and obscurity; or have been aggrieved by Fortune in some outrageous way. They have either been exposed to the mercy of wild beasts, or they have had so mean a parentage that in shame they have given themselves out to be sons of Jove or of some other deity. It would be wearisome to relate who these persons may have been because they are well known to everybody, and, as such tales would not be particularly edifying to those who read them, they are omitted. I believe that these lowly beginnings of great men occur because Fortune is desirous of showing to the world that such men owe much to her and little to wisdom, because she begins to show her hand when wisdom can really take no part in their career: thus all success must be attributed to her. Castruccio Castracani of Lucca was one of those men who did great deeds, if he is measured by the times in which he lived and the city in which he was born;

but, like many others, he was neither fortunate nor distinguished in his birth, as the course of this history will show. It appeared to be desirable to recall his memory, because I have discerned in him such indications of valour and fortune as should make him a great exemplar to men. I think also that I ought to call your attention to his actions, because you of all men I know delight most in noble deeds.

The family of Castracani was formerly numbered among the noble families of Lucca, but in the days of which I speak it had somewhat fallen in estate, as so often happens in this world. To this family was born a son Antonio, who became a priest of the order of San Michele of Lucca, and for this reason was honoured with the title of Messer Antonio. He had an only sister, who had been married to Buonaccorso Cenami, but Buonaccorso dying she became a widow, and not wishing to marry again went to live with her brother. Messer Antonio had a vineyard behind the house where he resided, and as it was bounded on all sides by gardens, any person could have access to it without difficulty. One morning, shortly after sunrise, Madonna Dianora, as the sister of Messer Antonio was called, had occasion to go into the vineyard as usual to gather herbs for seasoning the dinner, and hearing a slight rustling among the leaves of a vine she turned her eyes in that direction, and heard something resembling the cry of an infant. Whereupon she went towards it, and saw the hands and face of a baby who was lying enveloped in the leaves and who seemed to be crying for its mother. Partly wondering and partly fearing, yet full of compassion, she lifted it up and carried it to the house, where she washed it and clothed it with clean linen as is customary, and showed it to Messer Antonio when he returned home. When he heard what had happened and saw the child he was not less surprised or compassionate than his sister. They discussed between themselves what should be done, and seeing that he was priest and that she had no children, they finally determined to bring it up. They had a nurse for it, and it was reared and loved as if it were their own child. They baptized it, and gave it the name of Castruccio after their father. As the years passed Castruccio grew very handsome, and gave evidence of wit and discretion, and learnt with a quickness beyond his years those lessons which Messer Antonio imparted to him. Messer Antonio intended to make a priest of him, and in time would have inducted him into his canonry and other benefices, and all his instruction was given with this object; but Antonio discovered that the character of Castruccio was quite unfitted for the priesthood. As soon as Castruccio reached the age of fourteen he began to take less notice of the chiding of Messer Antonio and Madonna Dianora and no longer to fear them; he left off reading ecclesiastical books, and turned to playing with arms, delighting in nothing so much as in learning their uses, and in running, leaping, and wrestling with other boys. In all exercises he far excelled his companions in courage and bodily strength, and if at any time he did turn to books, only those pleased him which told of wars and the mighty deeds of men. Messer Antonio beheld all this with vexation and sorrow.

There lived in the city of Lucca a gentleman of the Guinigi family, named Messer Francesco, whose profession was arms and who in riches, bodily strength, and valour excelled all other men in Lucca. He had often fought under the command of the Visconti of Milan, and as a Ghibelline was the valued leader of that party in Lucca. This gentleman resided in Lucca and was accustomed to assemble with others most mornings and evenings under the balcony of the Podesta, which is at the top of the square of San Michele, the finest square in Lucca, and he had often seen Castruccio taking part with other children of the street in those games of which I have spoken. Noticing that Castruccio far excelled the other boys, and that he appeared to exercise a royal authority over them, and that they loved and obeyed him, Messer Francesco became greatly desirous of learning who he was. Being informed of the circumstances of the bringing up of Castruccio he felt a greater desire to have him near to him. Therefore he called him one day and asked him whether he would more willingly live in the house of a gentleman, where he would learn to ride horses and use arms, or in the house of a priest, where he would learn nothing but masses and the services of the Church. Messer Francesco could see that it pleased Castruccio greatly to hear horses and arms spoken of, even though he stood silent, blushing modestly; but being encouraged by Messer Francesco to speak, he answered that, if his master were agreeable, nothing would please him more than to give up his priestly studies and take up those of a soldier. This reply delighted Messer Francesco, and in a very short time he obtained the consent of Messer Antonio, who was driven to yield by his knowledge of the nature of the lad, and the fear that he would not be able to hold him much longer.

Thus Castruccio passed from the house of Messer Antonio the priest to the house of Messer Francesco Guinigi the soldier, and it was astonishing to find that in a very short time he manifested all that virtue and bearing which we are accustomed to associate with a true gentleman. In the first place he became an accomplished horseman, and could manage with ease the most fiery charger, and in all jousts and tournaments, although still a youth, he was observed beyond all others, and he excelled in all exercises of strength and dexterity. But what enhanced so much the charm of these accomplishments, was the delightful modesty which enabled him to avoid offence in either act or word to others, for he was deferential to the great men, modest with his equals, and courteous to his inferiors. These gifts made him beloved, not only by all the Guinigi family, but by all Lucca. When Castruccio had reached his eighteenth year, the Ghibellines were driven from Pavia by the Guelphs, and Messer Francesco was sent by the Visconti to assist the Ghibellines, and with him went Castruccio, in charge of his forces. Castruccio gave ample proof of his prudence and courage in this expedition, acquiring greater reputation than any other captain, and his name and fame were known, not only in Pavia, but throughout all Lombardy.

Castruccio, having returned to Lucca in far higher estimation than he left it, did not omit to use all the means in his power to gain as many friends as he could, neglecting none of those arts which are necessary for that purpose. About this time Messer Francesco died, leaving a son thirteen years of age named Pagolo, and having appointed Castruccio to be his son's tutor and administrator of his estate. Before he died Francesco called Castruccio to him, and prayed him to show Pagolo that goodwill which he (Francesco) had always shown to HIM, and to render to the son the gratitude which he had not been able to repay to the father. Upon the death of Francesco, Castruccio became the governor and tutor of Pagolo, which increased enormously his power and position, and created a certain amount of envy against him in Lucca in place of the former universal goodwill, for many men suspected him of harbouring tyrannical intentions. Among these the leading man was Giorgio degli Opizi, the head of the Guelph party. This man hoped after the death of Messer Francesco to become the chief man in Lucca, but it seemed to him that Castruccio, with the great abilities which he already showed, and holding the position of governor, deprived him of his opportunity; therefore he began to sow those seeds which should rob Castruccio of his eminence. Castruccio at first treated this with scorn, but afterwards he grew alarmed, thinking that Messer Giorgio might be able to bring him into disgrace with the deputy of King Ruberto of Naples and have him driven out of Lucca.

The Lord of Pisa at that time was Uguccione of the Faggiuola of Arezzo, who being in the first place elected their captain afterwards became their lord. There resided in Paris some exiled Ghibellines from Lucca, with whom Castruccio held communications with the object of effecting their restoration by the help of Uguccione. Castruccio also brought into his plans friends from Lucca who would not endure the authority of the Opizi. Having fixed upon a plan to be followed, Castruccio cautiously fortified the tower of the Onesti, filling it with supplies and munitions of war, in order that it might stand a siege for a few days in case of need. When the night came which had been agreed upon with Uguccione, who had occupied the plain between the mountains and Pisa with many men, the signal was given, and without being observed Uguccione approached the gate of San Piero and set fire to the portcullis. Castruccio raised a great uproar within the city, calling the people to arms and forcing open the gate from his side. Uguccione entered with his men, poured through the town, and killed Messer Giorgio with all his family and many of his friends and supporters. The governor was driven out, and the government reformed according to the wishes of Uguccione, to the detriment of the city, because it was found that more than one hundred families were exiled at that time. Of those who fled, part went to Florence and part to Pistoia, which city was the headquarters of the Guelph party, and for this reason it became most hostile to Uguccione and the Lucchese.

As it now appeared to the Florentines and others of the Guelph party that the Ghibellines absorbed too much power in Tuscany, they determined to restore the exiled Guelphs to Lucca. They assembled a large army in the Val di Nievole, and seized Montecatini; from thence they marched to Montecarlo, in order to secure the free passage into Lucca. Upon this Uguccione assembled his Pisan and Lucchese forces, and with a number of German cavalry which he drew out of Lombardy, he moved against the quarters of the Florentines, who upon the appearance of the enemy withdrew from Montecarlo, and posted themselves between Montecatini and Pescia. Uguccione now took up a position near to Montecarlo, and within about two miles of the enemy, and slight skirmishes between the horse of both parties were of daily occurrence. Owing to the illness of Uguccione, the Pisans and Lucchese delayed coming to battle with the enemy. Uguccione, finding himself growing worse, went to Montecarlo to be cured, and left the command of the army in the hands of Castruccio. This change brought about the ruin of the Guelphs, who, thinking that the hostile army having lost its captain had lost its head, grew over-confident. Castruccio observed this, and allowed some days to pass in order to encourage this belief; he also showed signs of fear, and did not allow any of the munitions of the camp to be used. On the other side, the Guelphs grew more insolent the more they saw these evidences of fear, and every day they drew out in the order of battle in front of the army of Castruccio. Presently, deeming that the enemy was sufficiently emboldened, and having mastered their tactics, he decided to join battle with them. First he spoke a few words of encouragement to his soldiers, and pointed out to them the certainty of victory if they would but obey his commands. Castruccio had noticed how the enemy had placed all his best troops in the centre of the line of battle, and his less reliable men on the wings of the army; whereupon he did exactly the opposite, putting his most valiant men on the flanks, while those on whom he could not so strongly rely he moved to the centre. Observing this order of battle, he drew out of his lines and quickly came in sight of the hostile army, who, as usual, had come in their insolence to defy him. He then commanded his centre squadrons to march slowly, whilst he moved rapidly forward those on the wings. Thus, when they came into contact with the enemy, only the wings of the two armies became engaged, whilst the center battalions remained out of action, for these two portions of the line of battle were separated from each other by a long interval and thus unable to reach each other. By this expedient the more valiant part of Castruccio's men were opposed to the weaker part of the enemy's troops, and the most efficient men of the enemy were disengaged; and thus the Florentines were unable to fight with those who were arrayed opposite to them, or to give any assistance to their own flanks. So, without much difficulty, Castruccio put the enemy to flight on both flanks, and the centre battalions took to flight when they found themselves exposed to attack, without having a chance of displaying their valour. The defeat was complete, and the loss in men very heavy, there being more than ten thousand men killed with many officers and knights of the Guelph party in Tuscany, and also many princes who had come to help them, among whom were Piero, the brother of King Ruberto, and Carlo, his nephew, and Filippo, the lord of Taranto. On the part of Castruccio the loss did not amount to more than three hundred men, among whom was Francesco, the son of Uguccione, who, being young and rash, was killed in the first onset.

This victory so greatly increased the reputation of Castruccio that Uguccione conceived some jealousy and suspicion of him, because it appeared to Uguccione that this victory had given him no increase of power, but rather than diminished it. Being of this mind, he only waited for an opportunity to give effect to it. This occurred on the death of Pier Agnolo Micheli, a man of great repute and abilities in Lucca, the murderer of whom fled to the house of Castruccio for refuge. On the sergeants of the captain going to arrest the murderer, they were driven off by Castruccio, and the murderer escaped. This affair coming to the knowledge of Uguccione, who was then at Pisa, it appeared to him a proper opportunity to punish Castruccio. He therefore sent for his son Neri, who was the governor of Lucca, and commissioned him to take Castruccio prisoner at a banquet and put him to death. Castruccio, fearing no evil, went to the governor in a friendly way, was entertained at supper, and then thrown into prison. But Neri, fearing to put him to death lest the people should be incensed, kept him alive, in order to hear further from his father concerning his intentions. Ugucionne cursed the hesitation and cowardice of his son, and at once set out from Pisa to Lucca with four hundred horsemen to finish the business in his own way; but he had not yet reached the baths when the Pisans rebelled and put his deputy to death and created Count Gaddo della Gherardesca their lord. Before Uguccione reached Lucca he heard of the occurrences at Pisa, but it did not appear wise to him to turn back, lest the Lucchese with the example of Pisa before them should close their gates against him. But the Lucchese, having heard of what had happened at Pisa, availed themselves of this opportunity to demand the liberation of Castruccio, notwithstanding that Uguccione had arrived in their city. They first began to speak of it in private circles, afterwards openly in the squares and streets; then they raised a tumult, and with arms in their hands went to Uguccione and demanded that Castruccio should be set at liberty. Uguccione, fearing that worse might happen, released him from prison. Whereupon Castruccio gathered his friends around him, and with the help of the people attacked Uguccione; who, finding he had no resource but in flight, rode away with his friends to Lombardy, to the lords of Scale, where he died in poverty.

But Castruccio from being a prisoner became almost a prince in Lucca, and he carried himself so discreetly with his friends and the people that they appointed him captain of their army for one year. Having obtained this, and wishing to gain renown in war, he planned the recovery of the many towns which had rebelled after the departure of Uguccione, and with the help of the Pisans, with whom he had concluded a treaty, he marched to Serezzana. To capture this place he constructed a fort against it, which is called to-day Zerezzanello; in the course of two months Castruccio captured the town. With the reputation gained at that siege, he rapidly seized Massa, Carrara, and Lavenza, and in a short time had overrun the whole of Lunigiana. In order to close the pass which leads from Lombardy to Lunigiana, he besieged Pontremoli and wrested it from the hands of Messer Anastagio Palavicini, who was the lord of it. After this victory he returned to Lucca, and was welcomed by the whole people. And now Castruccio, deeming it imprudent any longer to defer making himself a prince, got himself created the lord of Lucca by the help of Pazzino del Poggio, Puccinello dal Portico, Francesco Boccansacchi, and Cecco Guinigi, all of whom he had corrupted; and he was afterwards solemnly and deliberately elected prince by the people. At this time Frederick of Bavaria, the King of the Romans, came into Italy to assume the Imperial crown, and Castruccio, in order that he might make friends with him, met him at the head of five hundred horsemen. Castruccio had left as his deputy in Lucca, Pagolo Guinigi, who was held in high estimation, because of the people's love for the memory of his father. Castruccio was received in great honour by Frederick, and many privileges were conferred upon him, and he was appointed the emperor's lieutenant in Tuscany. At this time the Pisans were in great fear of Gaddo della Gherardesca, whom they had driven out of Pisa, and they had recourse for assistance to Frederick. Frederick created Castruccio the lord of Pisa, and the Pisans, in dread of the Guelph party, and particularly of the Florentines, were constrained to accept him as their lord.

Frederick, having appointed a governor in Rome to watch his Italian affairs, returned to Germany. All the Tuscan and Lombardian Ghibellines, who followed the imperial lead, had recourse to Castruccio for help and counsel, and all promised him the governorship of his country, if enabled to recover it with his assistance. Among these exiles were Matteo Guidi, Nardo Scolari, Lapo Uberti, Gerozzo Nardi, and Piero Buonaccorsi, all exiled Florentines and Ghibellines. Castruccio had the secret intention of becoming the master of all Tuscany by the aid of these men and of his own forces; and in order to gain greater weight in affairs, he entered into a league with Messer Matteo Visconti, the Prince of Milan, and organized for him the forces of his city and the country districts. As Lucca had five gates, he divided his own country districts into five parts, which he supplied with arms, and enrolled the men under captains and ensigns, so that he could quickly bring into the field twenty thousand soldiers, without those whom he could summon to his assistance from Pisa. While he surrounded himself with these forces and allies, it happened at Messer Matteo Visconti was attacked by the Guelphs of Piacenza, who had driven out the Ghibellines with the assistance of a Florentine army and the King Ruberto. Messer Matteo called upon Castruccio to invade the Florentines in their own territories, so that, being attacked at home, they should be compelled to draw their army out of Lombardy in order to defend themselves. Castruccio invaded the Valdarno, and seized Fucecchio and San Miniato, inflicting immense damage upon the country. Whereupon the Florentines recalled their army, which had scarcely reached Tuscany, when Castruccio was forced by other necessities to return to Lucca.

There resided in the city of Lucca the Poggio family, who were so powerful that they could not only elevate Castruccio, but even advance him to the dignity of prince; and it appearing to them they had not received such rewards for their services as they deserved, they incited other families to rebel and to drive Castruccio out of Lucca. They found their opportunity one morning, and arming themselves, they set upon the lieutenant whom Castruccio had left to maintain order and killed him. They endeavoured to raise the people in revolt, but Stefano di Poggio, a peaceable old man who had taken no hand in the rebellion, intervened and compelled them by his authority to lay down their arms; and he offered to be their mediator with Castruccio to obtain from him what they desired. Therefore they laid down their arms with no greater intelligence than they had taken them up. Castruccio, having heard the news of what had happened at Lucca, at once put Pagolo Guinigi in command of the army, and with a troop of cavalry set out for home. Contrary to his expectations, he found the rebellion at an end, yet he posted his men in the most advantageous places throughout the city. As it appeared to Stefano that Castruccio ought to be very much obliged to him, he sought him out, and without saying anything on his own behalf, for he did not recognize any need for doing so, he begged Castruccio to pardon the other members of his family by reason of their youth, their former friendships, and the obligations which Castruccio was under to their house. To this Castruccio graciously responded, and begged Stefano to reassure himself, declaring that it gave him more pleasure to find the tumult at an end than it had ever caused him anxiety to hear of its inception. He encouraged Stefano to bring his family to him, saying that he thanked God for having given him the opportunity of showing his clemency and liberality. Upon the word of Stefano and Castruccio they surrendered, and with Stefano were immediately thrown into prison and put to death. Meanwhile the Florentines had recovered San Miniato, whereupon it seemed advisable to Castruccio to make peace, as it did not appear to him that he was sufficiently secure at Lucca to leave him. He approached the Florentines with the proposal of a truce, which they readily entertained, for they were weary of the war, and desirous of getting rid of the expenses of it. A treaty was concluded with them for two years, by which both parties agreed to keep the conquests they had made. Castruccio thus released from this trouble, turned his attention to affairs in Lucca, and in order that he should not again be subject to the perils from which he had just escaped, he, under various pretences and reasons, first wiped out all those who by their ambition might aspire to the principality; not sparing one of them, but depriving them of country and property, and those whom he had in his hands of life also, stating that he had found by experience that none of them were to be trusted. Then for his further security he raised a fortress in Lucca with the stones of the towers of those whom he had killed or hunted out of the state.

Whilst Castruccio made peace with the Florentines, and strengthened his position in Lucca, he neglected no opportunity, short of open war, of increasing his importance elsewhere. It appeared to him that if he could get possession of Pistoia, he would have one foot in Florence, which was his great desire. He, therefore, in various ways made friends with the mountaineers, and worked matters so in Pistoia that both parties confided their secrets to him. Pistoia was divided, as it always had been, into the Bianchi and Neri parties; the head of the Bianchi was Bastiano di Possente, and of the Neri, Jacopo da Gia. Each of these men held secret communications with Castruccio, and each desired to drive the other out of the city; and, after many threatenings, they came to blows. Jacopo fortified himself at the Florentine gate, Bastiano at that of the Lucchese side of the city; both trusted more in Castruccio than in the Florentines, because they believed that Castruccio was far more ready and willing to fight than the Florentines, and they both sent to him for assistance. He gave promises to both, saying to Bastiano that he would come in person, and to Jacopo that he would send his pupil, Pagolo Guinigi. At the appointed time he sent forward Pagolo by way of Pisa, and went himself direct to Pistoia; at midnight both of them met outside the city, and both were admitted as friends. Thus the two leaders entered, and at a signal given by Castruccio, one killed Jacopo da Gia, and the other Bastiano di Possente, and both took prisoners or killed the partisans of either faction. Without further opposition Pistoia passed into the hands of Castruccio, who, having forced the Signoria to leave the palace, compelled the people to yield obedience to him, making them many promises and remitting their old debts. The countryside flocked to the city to see the new prince, and all were filled with hope and quickly settled down, influenced in a great measure by his great valour.

About this time great disturbances arose in Rome, owing to the dearness of living which was caused by the absence of the pontiff at Avignon. The German governor, Enrico, was much blamed for what happened—murders and tumults following each other daily, without his being able to put an end to them. This caused Enrico much anxiety lest the Romans should call in Ruberto, the King of Naples, who would drive the Germans out of the city, and bring back the Pope. Having no nearer friend to whom he could apply for help than Castruccio, he sent to him, begging him not only to give him assistance, but also to come in person to Rome. Castruccio considered that he ought not to hesitate to render the emperor this service, because he believed that he himself would not be safe if at any time the emperor ceased to hold Rome. Leaving Pagolo Guinigi in command at Lucca, Castruccio set out for Rome with six hundred horsemen, where he was received by Enrico with the greatest distinction. In a short time the presence of Castruccio obtained such respect for the emperor that, without bloodshed or violence, good order was restored, chiefly by reason of Castruccio having sent by sea from the country round Pisa large quantities of corn, and thus removed the source of the trouble. When he had chastised some of the Roman leaders, and admonished others, voluntary obedience was rendered to Enrico. Castruccio received many honours, and was made a Roman senator. This dignity was assumed with the greatest pomp, Castruccio being clothed in a brocaded toga, which had the following words embroidered on its front: "I am what God wills." Whilst on the back was: "What God desires shall be."

During this time the Florentines, who were much enraged that Castruccio should have seized Pistoia during the truce, considered how they could tempt the city to rebel, to do which they thought would not be difficult in his absence. Among the exiled Pistoians in Florence were Baldo Cecchi and Jacopo Baldini, both men of leading and ready to face danger. These men kept up communications with their friends in Pistoia, and with the aid of the Florentines entered the city by night, and after driving out some of Castruccio's officials and partisans, and killing others, they restored the city to its freedom. The news of this greatly angered Castruccio, and taking leave of Enrico, he pressed on in great haste to Pistoia. When the Florentines heard of his return, knowing that he would lose no time, they decided to intercept him with their forces in the Val di Nievole, under the belief that by doing so they would cut off his road to Pistoia. Assembling a great army of the supporters of the Guelph cause, the Florentines entered the Pistoian territories. On the other hand, Castruccio reached Montecarlo with his army; and having heard where the Florentines' lay, he decided not to encounter it in the plains of Pistoia, nor to await it in the plains of Pescia, but, as far as he possibly could, to attack it boldly in the Pass of Serravalle. He believed that if he succeeded in this design, victory was assured, although he was informed that the Florentines had thirty thousand men, whilst he had only twelve thousand. Although he had every confidence in his own abilities and the valour of his troops, yet he hesitated to attack his enemy in the open lest he should be overwhelmed by numbers. Serravalle is a castle between Pescia and Pistoia, situated on a hill which blocks the Val di Nievole, not in the exact pass, but about a bowshot beyond; the pass itself is in places narrow and steep, whilst in general it ascends gently, but is still narrow, especially at the summit where the waters divide, so that twenty men side by side could hold it. The lord of Serravalle was Manfred, a German, who, before Castruccio became lord of Pistoia, had been allowed to remain in possession of the castle, it being common to the Lucchese and the Pistoians, and unclaimed by either—neither of them wishing to displace Manfred as long as he kept his promise of neutrality, and came under obligations to no one. For these reasons, and also because the castle was well fortified, he had always been able to maintain his position. It was here that Castruccio had determined to fall upon his enemy, for here his few men would have the advantage, and there was no fear lest, seeing the large masses of the hostile force before they became engaged, they should not stand. As soon as this trouble with Florence arose, Castruccio saw the immense advantage which possession of this castle would give him, and having an intimate friendship with a resident in the castle, he managed matters so with him that four hundred of his men were to be admitted into the castle the night before the attack on the Florentines, and the castellan put to death.

Castruccio, having prepared everything, had now to encourage the Florentines to persist in their desire to carry the seat of war away from Pistoia into the Val di Nievole, therefore he did not move his army from Montecarlo. Thus the Florentines hurried on until they reached their encampment under Serravalle, intending to cross the hill on the following morning. In the meantime, Castruccio had seized the castle at night, had also moved his army from Montecarlo, and marching from thence at midnight in dead silence, had reached the foot of Serravalle: thus he and the Florentines commenced the ascent of the hill at the same time in the morning. Castruccio sent forward his infantry by the main road, and a troop of four hundred horsemen by a path on the left towards the castle. The Florentines sent forward four hundred cavalry ahead of their army which was following, never expecting to find Castruccio in possession of the hill, nor were they aware of his having seized the castle. Thus it happened that the Florentine horsemen mounting the hill were completely taken by surprise when they discovered the infantry of Castruccio, and so close were they upon it they had scarcely time to pull down their visors. It was a case of unready soldiers being attacked by ready, and they were assailed with such vigour that with difficulty they could hold their own, although some few of them got through. When the noise of the fighting reached the Florentine camp below, it was filled with confusion. The cavalry and infantry became inextricably mixed: the captains were unable to get their men either backward or forward, owing to the narrowness of the pass, and amid all this tumult no one knew what ought to be done or what could be done. In a short time the cavalry who were engaged with the enemy's infantry were scattered or killed without having made any effective defence because of their unfortunate position, although in sheer desperation they had offered a stout resistance. Retreat had been impossible, with the mountains on both flanks, whilst in front were their enemies, and in the rear their friends. When Castruccio saw that his men were unable to strike a decisive blow at the enemy and put them to flight, he sent one thousand infantrymen round by the castle, with orders to join the four hundred horsemen he had previously dispatched there, and commanded the whole force to fall upon the flank of the enemy. These orders they carried out with such fury that the Florentines could not sustain the attack, but gave way, and were soon in full retreat—conquered more by their unfortunate position than by the valour of their enemy. Those in the rear turned towards Pistoia, and spread through the plains, each man seeking only his own safety. The defeat was complete and very sanguinary. Many captains were taken prisoners, among whom were Bandini dei Rossi, Francesco Brunelleschi, and Giovanni della Tosa, all Florentine noblemen, with many Tuscans and Neapolitans who fought on the Florentine side, having been sent by King Ruberto to assist the Guelphs. Immediately the Pistoians heard of this defeat they drove out the friends of the Guelphs, and surrendered to Castruccio. He was not content with occupying Prato and all the castles on the plains on both sides of the Arno, but marched his army into the plain of Peretola, about two miles from Florence. Here he remained many days, dividing the spoils, and celebrating his victory with feasts and games, holding horse races, and foot races for men and women. He also struck medals in commemoration of the defeat of the Florentines.

He endeavoured to corrupt some of the citizens of Florence, who were to open the city gates at night; but the conspiracy was discovered, and the participators in it taken and beheaded, among whom were Tommaso Lupacci and Lambertuccio Frescobaldi. This defeat caused the Florentines great anxiety, and despairing of preserving their liberty, they sent envoys to King Ruberto of Naples, offering him the dominion of their city; and he, knowing of what immense importance the maintenance of the Guelph cause was to him, accepted it. He agreed with the Florentines to receive from them a yearly tribute of two hundred thousand florins, and he sent his son Carlo to Florence with four thousand horsemen.

Shortly after this the Florentines were relieved in some degree of the pressure of Castruccio's army, owing to his being compelled to leave his positions before Florence and march on Pisa, in order to suppress a conspiracy that had been raised against him by Benedetto Lanfranchi, one of the first men in Pisa, who could not endure that his fatherland should be under the dominion of the Lucchese. He had formed this conspiracy, intending to seize the citadel, kill the partisans of Castruccio, and drive out the garrison. As, however, in a conspiracy paucity of numbers is essential to secrecy, so for its execution a few are not sufficient, and in seeking more adherents to his conspiracy Lanfranchi encountered a person who revealed the design to Castruccio. This betrayal cannot be passed by without severe reproach to Bonifacio Cerchi and Giovanni Guidi, two Florentine exiles who were suffering their banishment in Pisa. Thereupon Castruccio seized Benedetto and put him to death, and beheaded many other noble citizens, and drove their families into exile. It now appeared to Castruccio that both Pisa and Pistoia were thoroughly disaffected; he employed much thought and energy upon securing his position there, and this gave the Florentines their opportunity to reorganize their army, and to await the coming of Carlo, the son of the King of Naples. When Carlo arrived they decided to lose no more time, and assembled a great army of more than thirty thousand infantry and ten thousand cavalry—having called to their aid every Guelph there was in Italy. They consulted whether they should attack Pistoia or Pisa first, and decided that it would be better to march on the latter—a course, owing to the recent conspiracy, more likely to succeed, and of more advantage to them, because they believed that the surrender of Pistoia would follow the acquisition of Pisa.

In the early part of May 1328, the Florentines put in motion this army and quickly occupied Lastra, Signa, Montelupo, and Empoli, passing from thence on to San Miniato. When Castruccio heard of the enormous army which the Florentines were sending against him, he was in no degree alarmed, believing that the time had now arrived when Fortune would deliver the empire of Tuscany into his hands, for he had no reason to think that his enemy would make a better fight, or had better prospects of success, than at Pisa or Serravalle. He assembled twenty thousand foot soldiers and four thousand horsemen, and with this army went to Fucecchio, whilst he sent Pagolo Guinigi to Pisa with five thousand infantry. Fucecchio has a stronger position than any other town in the Pisan district, owing to its situation between the rivers Arno and Gusciana and its slight elevation above the surrounding plain. Moreover, the enemy could not hinder its being victualled unless they divided their forces, nor could they approach it either from the direction of Lucca or Pisa, nor could they get through to Pisa, or attack Castruccio's forces except at a disadvantage. In one case they would find themselves placed between his two armies, the one under his own command and the other under Pagolo, and in the other case they would have to cross the Arno to get to close quarters with the enemy, an undertaking of great hazard. In order to tempt the Florentines to take this latter course, Castruccio withdrew his men from the banks of the river and placed them under the walls of Fucecchio, leaving a wide expanse of land between them and the river.

The Florentines, having occupied San Miniato, held a council of war to decide whether they should attack Pisa or the army of Castruccio, and, having weighed the difficulties of both courses, they decided upon the latter. The river Arno was at that time low enough to be fordable, yet the water reached to the shoulders of the infantrymen and to the saddles of the horsemen. On the morning of 10 June 1328, the Florentines commenced the battle by ordering forward a number of cavalry and ten thousand infantry. Castruccio, whose plan of action was fixed, and who well knew what to do, at once attacked the Florentines with five thousand infantry and three thousand horsemen, not allowing them to issue from the river before he charged them; he also sent one thousand light infantry up the river bank, and the same number down the Arno. The infantry of the Florentines were so much impeded by their arms and the water that they were not able to mount the banks of the river, whilst the cavalry had made the passage of the river more difficult for the others, by reason of the few who had crossed having broken up the bed of the river, and this being deep with mud, many of the horses rolled over with their riders and many of them had stuck so fast that they could not move. When the Florentine captains saw the difficulties their men were meeting, they withdrew them and moved higher up the river, hoping to find the river bed less treacherous and the banks more adapted for landing. These men were met at the bank by the forces which Castruccio had already sent forward, who, being light armed with bucklers and javelins in their hands, let fly with tremendous shouts into the faces and bodies of the cavalry. The horses, alarmed by the noise and the wounds, would not move forward, and trampled each other in great confusion. The fight between the men of Castruccio and those of the enemy who succeeded in crossing was sharp and terrible; both sides fought with the utmost desperation and neither would yield. The soldiers of Castruccio fought to drive the others back into the river, whilst the Florentines strove to get a footing on land in order to make room for the others pressing forward, who if they could but get out of the water would be able to fight, and in this obstinate conflict they were urged on by their captains. Castruccio shouted to his men that these were the same enemies whom they had before conquered at Serravalle, whilst the Florentines reproached each other that the many should be overcome by the few. At length Castruccio, seeing how long the battle had lasted, and that both his men and the enemy were utterly exhausted, and that both sides had many killed and wounded, pushed forward another body of infantry to take up a position at the rear of those who were fighting; he then commanded these latter to open their ranks as if they intended to retreat, and one part of them to turn to the right and another to the left. This cleared a space of which the Florentines at once took advantage, and thus gained possession of a portion of the battlefield. But when these tired soldiers found themselves at close quarters with Castruccio's reserves they could not stand against them and at once fell back into the river. The cavalry of either side had not as yet gained any decisive advantage over the other, because Castruccio, knowing his inferiority in this arm, had commanded his leaders only to stand on the defensive against the attacks of their adversaries, as he hoped that when he had overcome the infantry he would be able to make short work of the cavalry. This fell out as he had hoped, for when he saw the Florentine army driven back across the river he ordered the remainder of his infantry to attack the cavalry of the enemy. This they did with lance and javelin, and, joined by their own cavalry, fell upon the enemy with the greatest fury and soon put him to flight. The Florentine captains, having seen the difficulty their cavalry had met with in crossing the river, had attempted to make their infantry cross lower down the river, in order to attack the flanks of Castruccio's army. But here, also, the banks were steep and already lined by the men of Castruccio, and this movement was quite useless. Thus the Florentines were so completely defeated at all points that scarcely a third of them escaped, and Castruccio was again covered with glory. Many captains were taken prisoners, and Carlo, the son of King Ruberto, with Michelagnolo Falconi and Taddeo degli Albizzi, the Florentine commissioners, fled to Empoli. If the spoils were great, the slaughter was infinitely greater, as might be expected in such a battle. Of the Florentines there fell twenty thousand two hundred and thirty-one men, whilst Castruccio lost one thousand five hundred and seventy men.

But Fortune growing envious of the glory of Castruccio took away his life just at the time when she should have preserved it, and thus ruined all those plans which for so long a time he had worked to carry into effect, and in the successful prosecution of which nothing but death could have stopped him. Castruccio was in the thick of the battle the whole of the day; and when the end of it came, although fatigued and overheated, he stood at the gate of Fucecchio to welcome his men on their return from victory and personally thank them. He was also on the watch for any attempt of the enemy to retrieve the fortunes of the day; he being of the opinion that it was the duty of a good general to be the first man in the saddle and the last out of it. Here Castruccio stood exposed to a wind which often rises at midday on the banks of the Arno, and which is often very unhealthy; from this he took a chill, of which he thought nothing, as he was accustomed to such troubles; but it was the cause of his death. On the following night he was attacked with high fever, which increased so rapidly that the doctors saw it must prove fatal. Castruccio, therefore, called Pagolo Guinigi to him, and addressed him as follows:

"If I could have believed that Fortune would have cut me off in the midst of the career which was leading to that glory which all my successes promised, I should have laboured less, and I should have left thee, if a smaller state, at least with fewer enemies and perils, because I should have been content with the governorships of Lucca and Pisa. I should neither have subjugated the Pistoians, nor outraged the Florentines with so many injuries. But I would have made both these peoples my friends, and I should have lived, if no longer, at least more peacefully, and have left you a state without a doubt smaller, but one more secure and established on a surer foundation. But Fortune, who insists upon having the arbitrament of human affairs, did not endow me with sufficient judgment to recognize this from the first, nor the time to surmount it. Thou hast heard, for many have told thee, and I have never concealed it, how I entered the house of thy father whilst yet a boy—a stranger to all those ambitions which every generous soul should feel—and how I was brought up by him, and loved as though I had been born of his blood; how under his governance I learned to be valiant and capable of availing myself of all that fortune, of which thou hast been witness. When thy good father came to die, he committed thee and all his possessions to my care, and I have brought thee up with that love, and increased thy estate with that care, which I was bound to show. And in order that thou shouldst not only possess the estate which thy father left, but also that which my fortune and abilities have gained, I have never married, so that the love of children should never deflect my mind from that gratitude which I owed to the children of thy father. Thus I leave thee a vast estate, of which I am well content, but I am deeply concerned, inasmuch as I leave it thee unsettled and insecure. Thou hast the city of Lucca on thy hands, which will never rest contented under thy government. Thou hast also Pisa, where the men are of nature changeable and unreliable, who, although they may be sometimes held in subjection, yet they will ever disdain to serve under a Lucchese. Pistoia is also disloyal to thee, she being eaten up with factions and deeply incensed against thy family by reason of the wrongs recently inflicted upon them. Thou hast for neighbours the offended Florentines, injured by us in a thousand ways, but not utterly destroyed, who will hail the news of my death with more delight than they would the acquisition of all Tuscany. In the Emperor and in the princes of Milan thou canst place no reliance, for they are far distant, slow, and their help is very long in coming. Therefore, thou hast no hope in anything but in thine own abilities, and in the memory of my valour, and in the prestige which this latest victory has brought thee; which, as thou knowest how to use it with prudence, will assist thee to come to terms with the Florentines, who, as they are suffering under this great defeat, should be inclined to listen to thee. And whereas I have sought to make them my enemies, because I believed that war with them would conduce to my power and glory, thou hast every inducement to make friends of them, because their alliance will bring thee advantages and security. It is of the greatest important in this world that a man should know himself, and the measure of his own strength and means; and he who knows that he has not a genius for fighting must learn how to govern by the arts of peace. And it will be well for thee to rule thy conduct by my counsel, and to learn in this way to enjoy what my life-work and dangers have gained; and in this thou wilt easily succeed when thou hast learnt to believe that what I have told thee is true. And thou wilt be doubly indebted to me, in that I have left thee this realm and have taught thee how to keep it."

After this there came to Castruccio those citizens of Pisa, Pistoia, and Lucca, who had been fighting at his side, and whilst recommending Pagolo to them, and making them swear obedience to him as his successor, he died. He left a happy memory to those who had known him, and no prince of those times was ever loved with such devotion as he was. His obsequies were celebrated with every sign of mourning, and he was buried in San Francesco at Lucca. Fortune was not so friendly to Pagolo Guinigi as she had been to Castruccio, for he had not the abilities. Not long after the death of Castruccio, Pagolo lost Pisa, and then Pistoia, and only with difficulty held on to Lucca. This latter city continued in the family of Guinigi until the time of the great-grandson of Pagolo.

From what has been related here it will be seen that Castruccio was a man of exceptional abilities, not only measured by men of his own time, but also by those of an earlier date. In stature he was above the ordinary height, and perfectly proportioned. He was of a gracious presence, and he welcomed men with such urbanity that those who spoke with him rarely left him displeased. His hair was inclined to be red, and he wore it cut short above the ears, and, whether it rained or snowed, he always went without a hat. He was delightful among friends, but terrible to his enemies; just to his subjects; ready to play false with the unfaithful, and willing to overcome by fraud those whom he desired to subdue, because he was wont to say that it was the victory that brought the glory, not the methods of achieving it. No one was bolder in facing danger, none more prudent in extricating himself. He was accustomed to say that men ought to attempt everything and fear nothing; that God is a lover of strong men, because one always sees that the weak are chastised by the strong. He was also wonderfully sharp or biting though courteous in his answers; and as he did not look for any indulgence in this way of speaking from others, so he was not angered with others did not show it to him. It has often happened that he has listened quietly when others have spoken sharply to him, as on the following occasions. He had caused a ducat to be given for a partridge, and was taken to task for doing so by a friend, to whom Castruccio had said: "You would not have given more than a penny." "That is true," answered the friend. Then said Castruccio to him: "A ducat is much less to me." Having about him a flatterer on whom he had spat to show that he scorned him, the flatterer said to him: "Fisherman are willing to let the waters of the sea saturate them in order that they may take a few little fishes, and I allow myself to be wetted by spittle that I may catch a whale"; and this was not only heard by Castruccio with patience but rewarded. When told by a priest that it was wicked for him to live so sumptuously, Castruccio said: "If that be a vice then you should not fare so splendidly at the feasts of our saints." Passing through a street he saw a young man as he came out of a house of ill fame blush at being seen by Castruccio, and said to him: "Thou shouldst not be ashamed when thou comest out, but when thou goest into such places." A friend gave him a very curiously tied knot to undo and was told: "Fool, do you think that I wish to untie a thing which gave so much trouble to fasten." Castruccio said to one who professed to be a philosopher: "You are like the dogs who always run after those who will give them the best to eat," and was answered: "We are rather like the doctors who go to the houses of those who have the greatest need of them." Going by water from Pisa to Leghorn, Castruccio was much disturbed by a dangerous storm that sprang up, and was reproached for cowardice by one of those with him, who said that he did not fear anything. Castruccio answered that he did not wonder at that, since every man valued his soul for what is was worth. Being asked by one what he ought to do to gain estimation, he said: "When thou goest to a banquet take care that thou dost not seat one piece of wood upon another." To a person who was boasting that he had read many things, Castruccio said: "He knows better than to boast of remembering many things." Someone bragged that he could drink much without becoming intoxicated. Castruccio replied: "An ox does the same." Castruccio was acquainted with a girl with whom he had intimate relations, and being blamed by a friend who told him that it was undignified for him to be taken in by a woman, he said: "She has not taken me in, I have taken her." Being also blamed for eating very dainty foods, he answered: "Thou dost not spend as much as I do?" and being told that it was true, he continued: "Then thou art more avaricious than I am gluttonous." Being invited by Taddeo Bernardi, a very rich and splendid citizen of Luca, to supper, he went to the house and was shown by Taddeo into a chamber hung with silk and paved with fine stones representing flowers and foliage of the most beautiful colouring. Castruccio gathered some saliva in his mouth and spat it out upon Taddeo, and seeing him much disturbed by this, said to him: "I knew not where to spit in order to offend thee less." Being asked how Caesar died he said: "God willing I will die as he did." Being one night in the house of one of his gentlemen where many ladies were assembled, he was reproved by one of his friends for dancing and amusing himself with them more than was usual in one of his station, so he said: "He who is considered wise by day will not be considered a fool at night." A person came to demand a favour of Castruccio, and thinking he was not listening to his plea threw himself on his knees to the ground, and being sharply reproved by Castruccio, said: "Thou art the reason of my acting thus for thou hast thy ears in thy feet," whereupon he obtained double the favour he had asked. Castruccio used to say that the way to hell was an easy one, seeing that it was in a downward direction and you travelled blindfolded. Being asked a favour by one who used many superfluous words, he said to him: "When you have another request to make, send someone else to make it." Having been wearied by a similar man with a long oration who wound up by saying: "Perhaps I have fatigued you by speaking so long," Castruccio said: "You have not, because I have not listened to a word you said." He used to say of one who had been a beautiful child and who afterwards became a fine man, that he was dangerous, because he first took the husbands from the wives and now he took the wives from their husbands. To an envious man who laughed, he said: "Do you laugh because you are successful or because another is unfortunate?" Whilst he was still in the charge of Messer Francesco Guinigi, one of his companions said to him: "What shall I give you if you will let me give you a blow on the nose?" Castruccio answered: "A helmet." Having put to death a citizen of Lucca who had been instrumental in raising him to power, and being told that he had done wrong to kill one of his old friends, he answered that people deceived themselves; he had only killed a new enemy. Castruccio praised greatly those men who intended to take a wife and then did not do so, saying that they were like men who said they would go to sea, and then refused when the time came. He said that it always struck him with surprise that whilst men in buying an earthen or glass vase would sound it first to learn if it were good, yet in choosing a wife they were content with only looking at her. He was once asked in what manner he would wish to be buried when he died, and answered: "With the face turned downwards, for I know when I am gone this country will be turned upside down." On being asked if it had ever occurred to him to become a friar in order to save his soul, he answered that it had not, because it appeared strange to him that Fra Lazerone should go to Paradise and Uguccione della Faggiuola to the Inferno. He was once asked when should a man eat to preserve his health, and replied: "If the man be rich let him eat when he is hungry; if he be poor, then when he can."

Seeing one of his gentlemen make a member of his family lace him up, he said to him: "I pray God that you will let him feed you also." Seeing that someone had written upon his house in Latin the words: "May God preserve this house from the wicked," he said, "The owner must never go in." Passing through one of the streets he saw a small house with a very large door, and remarked: "That house will fly through the door." He was having a discussion with the ambassador of the King of Naples concerning the property of some banished nobles, when a dispute arose between them, and the ambassador asked him if he had no fear of the king. "Is this king of yours a bad man or a good one?" asked Castruccio, and was told that he was a good one, whereupon he said, "Why should you suggest that I should be afraid of a good man?"

I could recount many other stories of his sayings both witty and weighty, but I think that the above will be sufficient testimony to his high qualities. He lived forty-four years, and was in every way a prince. And as he was surrounded by many evidences of his good fortune, so he also desired to have near him some memorials of his bad fortune; therefore the manacles with which he was chained in prison are to be seen to this day fixed up in the tower of his residence, where they were placed by him to testify forever to his days of adversity. As in his life he was inferior neither to Philip of Macedon, the father of Alexander, nor to Scipio of Rome, so he died in the same year of his age as they did, and he would doubtless have excelled both of them had Fortune decreed that he should be born, not in Lucca, but in Macedonia or Rome.

The End